Under His Protection

sarah Shah

Published by sarah Shah, 2023.

UNDER HIS PROTECTION

First edition. April 2, 2023.

ISBN: 979-8215979594

Written by sarah Shah.

Table of Contents

Chapter 1

L*ife truly is unexpected and unpredictable, who would have ever imagine being in this kind of situation?* Mitchie was tied up in a chair as she looked down sadly trying to fight back the tears in her eyes thinking, *'this is it; I am going to die here.'* An unknown person cocks a gun and points it at her asking, *"any last words?"* Mitchie wonders, *'last words? Is that necessary?'* Mitchie raises her eyes looking at the shooter replying, *"last words? Yes, I have my last words... GO TO HELL!."* The unknown assassin says, *"Goodbye, Mitchie Torres!"*. Mitchie closes her eyes as she thinks, *'I should probably start my story from the beginning and how I ended up in this situation'.* Our story begins in Tennessee where a young girl is playing the xylophone and sings a few lyrics of *'Heart and Soul';* her mother Kaitlyn says, *"very nice sweetheart, you will grow to be a famous musician"*. Mitchie smiles happily as she grows happily narrating *'singing has always been my passion, my love and the only thing I can do in my life.'* In a concert in New York City Mitchie remembers her mother's wise words, *'if there is one thing you can do it to perfection, focus on what you do best!.'*

Mitchie finishes a concert as she holds a frame photo of her mom Kaitlyn who was pregnant with her and her twin brother. Mitchie says, *"we never knew our father's identity, rumors said that she had an affair we her fan due to her love for him, but no one can prove this".* Mitchie remembers a memory when she found her mom was stabbed and left to bleed; Mitchie without a doubt had a suspect in her mind which was her dad. Mitchie thinks back to the past, *'I was only three years old when I saw my mom's body bleeding out'.* Kaitlyn's mom and dad came to visit and took the kids while calling the police and ambulance however the media soon found out about Kaitlyn's death, and it soon spread like wildfire calling it a *'murder mystery sensation'*. As Mitchie grew up with her brother Darren they always heard on Instagram and TikTok about their mom's death. Their grandfather Harry says, *"Mitchie, Darren don't look into the internet and the news a lot, they are full of lies".* Mitchie decided to not look anymore into the news as it just made her and her family feel sad regardless whether it was about them or not. At the age of twelve Mitchie decided to follow in her mother's footstep and try out for a career in singing while Darren decided to take the performing arts route and become an actor.

Mitchie grew up using music to convey her feelings. Soon on her way over for recording two guys noticed her saying, *"Mitchie Torres?! W-we are big fans."* His friend Mark next to him says, *"w-wow Mitchie in the flesh."* Joanna says, *"sorry, Mitchie is very busy right now".* Alex says, *"but, can we talk with you more, Mitchie? Please.... Please...please...,"* a young girl takes out her phone saying, *"Mitchie, look this way!."* Mark asks, *"can I have your autograph?".* Joanna says, *"please, Mitchie is very busy right now.. please excuse us."* Alex begs with his hand folded saying, *"please Mitchie, I bought all of your albums, atleast just a little talk with me?".* Mitchie smiles thinking, *'aww, my beloved fans without their support I'm just nobody'.* Mitchie waves saying, *"hello, you two thank you for supporting me, it means the world to me, without your support I wouldn't be what I am right now".* Alex says, *"wow, just like everyone said Mitchie Torres is so lovely and passionate".* Mark says, *"and her voice is so angelic".* Mitchie wonders, *'having my fans around me, interacting with them, nothing could be more perfect and comforting than this moment'.* Alex says, *"Mitchie, I have one question that hangs in my head for so long, do you enjoy rock music?".* Mitchie replies, *"rock is not my genre but I love it!".* Alex smiles saying, *"you are truly a sweet and innocent person who knows nothing but sugar and cakes".* One girl comes over with her book asking, *"Mitchie, can I ask for your autograph?".* Suddenly a crowd gathers screaming, *"MITCHIE TORRES!".* Joanna whispers to Mitchie, *"run!".* They both head off as Mitchie thinks, *'I am so used to this scene since I was young, it's nothing new to me.'* Later Mitchie has a TV interview as James says, *"so Miss Mitchie, do you have any plans for the future? A new song perhaps?"* Mitchie replies, *"hmm... a new song... of course! I am excited to work on a new album."* Mark says, *"we have HBO here, did you see the news? Everyone wants a collaboration between you two."* Jeremey says, *"I don't mind, I think it will be an exciting collaboration if it happens."* Mitchie thinks smiling, *'a collab with HBO sounds amazing!'.* Daniel says, *"you see, my director wanted Mitchie to be my co-star in 'Love Through Time' but sadly, Mitchie rejected it".* James says, *"but, it was a fantastic romantic movie, why did you reject it, Mitchie?".* Mitchie looks at James replying, *"I only live for music, not acting...."* She turns to Daniel apologizing and says, *"perhaps next time".* Daniel was understanding saying, *"of course, that is totally ok".*

Chapter 2

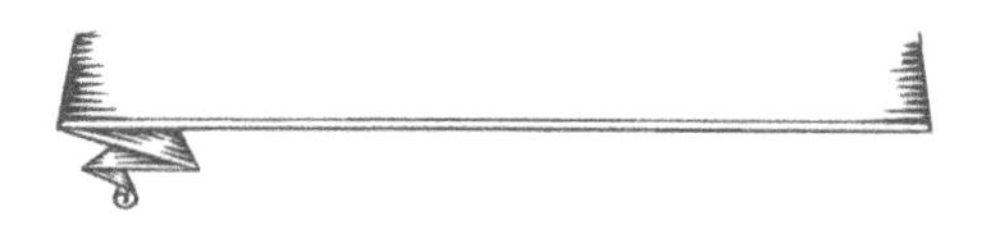

Mitchie wonders, *'I don't understand why everyone wants a little piece of me, but it's fun to have many people around you and wants to be your friend'.* Later that evening Mitchie was preparing herself for her concert. Kirsty says, *"alright, your hair and makeup is done, so? Are you ready for your concert?"*. Mitchie replies, *"I am so ready! I cannot wait to see all my fans! Thank you for your amazing hair and makeup as always, Kirsty."* Joanna comes saying, *"it's time to change your dress, Mitchie, come on we don't have much time"*. Mitchie looks at her options before choosing a silver goddess sparkly dress. She looks in the mirror thinking, *'even though I am a pop idol I can't lie that country has my go-to music'.* Joanna says, *"Mitchie, you have a gift from your fan"*. Mitchie is surprised seeing the small bouquet of flowers however just as she is about to take it; Joanna says, *"you will check this gift later after your concert, ok?."* Mitchie says, *"aww, I love the flowers, but you are right, after my concert"*. Joanna says, *"let's go! It's time!"* Soon Mitchie sang her heart out as the crowd danced and moved to the rhythm; two girls in particular were enjoying the show just as a guy came over saying, *"Miss Alexandra, we have to go now"*. Alexandra sighs saying, *"ugh, fine"*. A few moments later the concert finished as Joanna says, *"you were amazing, Mitchie! That is one of the best concerts from you!"*.

Mitchie smiles happily while Joanna checks her tablet for a moment before saying, *"you have to greet your VIP fans."* A crowd soon gathers around her with notepads asking, *"Mitchie, can I get your autograph?"*. The crowd begins to get bigger until Mitchie is knocked back and bumps into someone. She looks at the mysterious stranger who helps her up asking, *"are you ok?"*. Mitchie replies nervously, *"oh, umm.... I'm ok thank you so much for helping me!."* Joanna tries to settle the crowd saying, *"everyone, please calm down!"*. The mysterious stranger says, *"go."* Mitchie says, *"go? where?"* He says, *"people are waiting for you"*. Mitchie looks at him asking, *"hmmm, I have never seen you around, who are you?"*. He replies, *"someone who is not important, I guess"*.

Mitchie says, *"don't say that, everyone is important"*. He says, *"maybe but Miss if you have no more issues, I need to go now."* Mitchie wonders, *'so quiet, so cold, so mysterious... I have never met someone like this before, he's totally my type! Is this love at first sight? This is my chance....'* Mitchie says, *"so? Did you enjoy my concert? Huh? No answer? Would you like my autograph or a picture with me? We can take a picture or a short video together."* Mitchie notices the guy staring at her thinking, *'what happened to him?! Is he alright?'* Mitchie waves her hand asking, *"hello, hey are you ok?."* He finally speaks saying, *"you talk a lot, huh?"*. Mitchie is stunned while the mysterious stranger asks, *"why don't you sing something for me? you're a singer, right?"*. Mitchie nods and smile replying, *"ok, I will sing something for you"*. She takes a deep breath before singing, *"Oh, you must be my lucky star, cause you shine on me wherever you are, I just think of you and I start to glow, And I need your love, so baby, you know"*. Mitchie finishes saying, *"what do you think?"*. He ponders for a moment before answering, *"I think that was really sweet, what song is that?"*. Mitchie was stunned saying, *"you don't know? I thought you are my fan..."* He gives her a serious look as Mitchie rolls her eyes sighing saying, *"okay, it's my fault, I took it the wrong way, you are not my fan, sorry!"*. He casually and calmly says, *"it's cool, no worries"*. Mitchie again apologizes saying, *"sorry I wasted your time, but thanks for helping me up"*. Just then Alexandra comes asking, *"where is my bodyguard?!"*. Alexandra sees Mitchie saying, *"oh, nice concert by the way Mitchie!"*. She leaves as the guy follows her as Mitchie thinks,

'Alexandra Gibson likes my concert! and that's her bodyguard....' A guy comes over to her saying, *"hi Mitchie, my name's Wayne and I am your biggest fan!"*. Mitchie says, *"hello Wayne, nice to meet you".* Joanna soon calls out, *"Mitchie, we need you here!".* Mitchie comes back saying, *"I'm here! Sorry for waiting, everyone."* Soon after in her dressing room Mitchie yawns exhausted as Joanna says, *"I am going to get your car ready to go home, you must be tired."* Mitchie says, *"thank you so much, Joanna".* Joanna leaves as Mitchie sees the bouquet on the table saying, *"well time to check my fan mail!".* She sees a small envelope in the flower and opens it reading, *"dear, Miss Torres congratulations for your concert, do you remember your mother's murder case? Kaitlyn Torres's case? That's right... I am the one who is responsible for that incident, and I can see you have grown into a wonderful celebrity like your mother, you must miss your mother but don't worry... you will see her soon because I have a surprise for you... your secret admirer."* Mitchie drops the note in shock thinking, *'oh dear... it's a threat letter!'*

Chapter 3

Mitchie dropped the letter in shock still thinking, *'oh no, it's a threat letter... and it's.....connected to my mom's murderer? What should I do?.'* Joanna soon comes back as Mitchie picks up the letter and hides it; Joanna says, *"the car will be arriving soon."* Joanna notices Mitchie looking a little pale and lost in deep thoughts asking, *"Mitchie? Are you ok?."* Mitchie rubs her arm gently replying nervously, *"well....."* She wonders for a moment thinking, *'I can't let Joanna know... she will be worried.'* Mitchie sighs saying, *"it's nothing, I am just feeling hungry that's all, everything is fine Jo".* Joanna asks, *"are you sure?."* Mitchie replies, *"well.... I'm totally fine, Jo and I just need to eat and rest."* Joanna says, *"I will get you something to drink."* She leaves the room as Mitchie turns to look at the mirror just as her phone beeps and she sees an incoming message from an unknown number; she opens the text reading, *'hello, Mitchie.'* Mitchie texts, *'who is this?.'* The unknown person texts, *'did you like my letter? anyway, you should leave the building now if you value your life, because the game starts now.'* Mitchie was confused texting, *'what do you mean?! what do you want from me? ANSWER ME!.'*

Mitchie holds her phone in a worrying state wondering, *'what was that supposed to mean?.'* Just then there is an explosion as Mitchie looks at the flames spreading in the room; she is panicked by this saying, *"oh no! I need to escape from here!."* She tries to turn to the other corner however there is another explosion, and the flames begin to grow deeper. Mitchie thinks, *'oh no! I'm trapped! I need to do something;*

I need to let someone know that I am here and need some help!.' Unexpectedly outside the mysterious guy is near the door as Mitchie screams, *"HELP! HELP! ANYONE OUT THERE?!."* She coughs due the smoke as the door is kicked down and the mysterious guy asks, *"are you okay?!."* Mitchie was surprised to see him saying stunned, *"YOU!."* He runs to her saying, *"we have to leave and go now!."* Mitchie asks, *"why are you here?!."* She coughs again as the mysterious guys looks at her replying, *"does it matter? hold my hand! I will protect you!."* He extends his hand to her as Mitchie takes it and they run out of the room into the corridor which is blazing with smoke and flames; Mitchie coughs and soon collapses to the ground as the guy says, *"hey!."* He bends down and holds her close saying, *"hey, don't die on me, I am going to save you."* He gives her CPR as she coughs a little and then lifts her in his arms saying, *"I will not lie you die!."* Soon outside Mitchie is placed on a stretcher with two paramedics while the mysterious guy watches on just as Joanna comes dropping the juice and snack saying, *"OMG! Mitchie!."* The mysterious guy says, *"she is fine, don't worry."* Joanna looks at the guy asking, *"you saved her, didn't you? thank you so much, thank you! thank you!."* The guy smiles at her while Mitchie soon opens her eyes thinking, *'I can hear Joanna and.... my saviour.'* She feels the pain in her body weakly thinking, *'he's the one who saved my life, he may disappear at any moment, it's my only chance to thank him'.* Mitchie says, *"hey, can you hear me? t-thank you for saving my me, I thought I was going to die."*

The mysterious guy comes over and bends down saying, *"no worries, it's alright you don't need to thank me, it is normal for human beings to help each other, you don't owe me anything."* Mitchie says, *"n-no, please tell me what I can do to repay you, I do not know if I will see you again."* The mysterious guy replies, *"nothing, just stay and be safe."* Mitchie asks, *"will we see each other again? I still need to know about my saviour's identity?."* He replies, *"that is not important right now, if destiny allows it we will meet again."* Mitchie ponders in her mind, *'perhaps I should ask him his name so I can look for him later....'* Mitchie asks, *"m-may I ask for your name, please?."* He replies, *"Shane."* Mitchie says, *"t-thank you, Shane I hope we can meet again... t-thank you...."* Shane says, *"you are welcome."* Mitchie slowly closes her eyes and is escorted into the ambulance which soon drives off to the hospital. Joanna says, *"thank you again for saving Mitchie, we owe you one."* The car arrives which takes Joanna to the hospital; the next day Mitchie thinks, *'uugh....my head... my body.'* Joanna notices Mitchie stirring saying, *"Mitchie! Mitchie, are you okay?!."* Mitchie wakes up saying, *"uhhh..., my head and body ache."*

Chapter 4

Joanna asks, *"how are you feeling, Mitchie?."* Mitchie asks, *"uhhh... where am I? gosh, I am so hungry...I have a craving for dumplings".* Joanna says, *"I will go get the doctor for you!".* She runs out as Mitchie thinks sadly, *'I miss my own bed.....'* A few moment later the doctor comes in and runs some test on Mitchie who then says, *"you are doing very well, Miss Torres."* Mitchie smiles saying, *"finally, thank you doctor!."* The doctor laughs as Mitchie says, *"it's something that I needed to hear".* Joanna asks, *"so, can she go home today, doctor?".* The doctor replies, *"yes, of course I will leave you two alone".* Joanna comes over saying, *"you should take a long break."* Mitchie says, *"you are right, I may need a break but still I have a tight schedule".* Joanna says, *"so, Mitchie... how did this fire happen? did you know anything about it? I am so sorry I was not beside you when that happened".* Joanna hands Mitchie a glass of water as she drinks it thinking, *'Joanna is taking care of me all the time, it's important for her to raise the sense of awareness, the same thing has happened before and Joanna had a nice deal with that, so I bet if I let this go, my life will be under a huge threat'.* Mitchie places the water back down before saying, *"J-Joanna, you see, I... the flower... um.... I got hate mail; it was a threat letter. The letter also refer to my mother's death".* Joanna was stunned and shocked saying, *"OMG! that is so horrible! Where is the letter? Do you have it with you?".* Mitchie shakes her head replying, *"no, I left it in the dressing room, it should be nothing though".* Joanna was not convinced saying, *"but still, we should be wary now! people can be crazy, maybe it's just a one-time thing and you did nothing*

wrong, so it should be just someone that's jealous of you". Mitchie says, *"yeah, you're right I guess."* Joanna says, *"thanks for telling me, Mitchie."*

Just then a guy runs in wearing a devil costume screaming, *"MITCHIE!!! you are alive!."* Mitchie looks at the guy saying, *"oh, wow! hello, devil, what on earth are you wearing? you look cool by the way".* Darren replies, *"It's a costume for my upcoming movie 'Lucifer'... I was so worried about you?! I had no time to change, you are my one and only family member and I can't afford to lose you."* Someone comes behind him from the film set saying, *"Mr Torres, you cannot just leave the set like that! we are in the middle of shooting right now! the director will kill me".* Mitchie thinks, *'classic Darren, he is always so worried about me'.* Mitchie takes a deep breath before saying, *"Darren, you should go back to your set, I am fine... your film is very important, okay?!".* Darren says, *"you are more important than my film, sis".* The staff says, *"I will wait outside, just please make this quick."* Mitchie asks, *"anyway, did anyone check the news? I am worried and scared that someone gets hurt from the fire incident".* Joanna says, *"I think it's not a good idea to check on the news".* Darren says, *"I agree which is why I didn't bother to check the news too, it's not important or relevant.... news are never good."* Mitchie wonders, *'I have the worse anxiety... but... Darren and Joanna are right, I should ignore it.'* Joanna says, *"thankfully, nobody said anything bad but still, you need to focus on your health first".* Darren says, *"I should probably go now, the film crew and director must be angry with me however before I go, I have a surprise for you, sis"*. Mitchie smiles happily saying, *"ooh, I love surprises!".* Darren turns to the door saying, *"come out now!".* A guy walks in as Joanna and Mitchie both are stunned while Mitchie says still surprised, *"oh my god! YOU!."* Darren turns back to Mitchie confused asking, *"huh? you two know each other, sis?".* Mitchie replies, *"yes bro, he saved me! he is my saviour... I cannot believe we are meeting again."* Joanna says, *"what a destiny!."* Darren introduces him saying, *"he is Shane Gray! From now, he will be your bodyguard."* Mitchie says, *"my bodyguard?!.* Darren says, *"he has worked with Alexandra Gibson, that famous pop idol, he has a good reputation for this job".* Mitchie says, *"yes, I saw Alexandra Gibson at my concert... and Shane too".* Darren says, *"it's good if you both of you two know each other, easier to work together now".* Mitchie says, *"y-yes, I guess... it would be better to have someone you already know, I think but you see.... Darren, I don't need a bodyguard, I can take care of myself".*

Chapter 5

Darren looked at his sister firmly saying, *"nonsense, Mitchie! I cannot take care of you 24/7, you need a bodyguard, and I almost lost you, ok?! it's for your safety, sis".* Mitchie sighs saying, *"ok, I will listen to you".* Darren comes over and hugs her saying, *"perfect, I have to go now... bye Mitchie".* Darren turns to Shane saying, *"take care of my dear sister, ok?."* Shane nods as Darren runs out; Mitchie looks at Shane saying, *"you probably already know me but... I'm Mitchie, it's nice to meet you."* Shane doesn't respond and stares at her with his arms folded as Mitchie says, *"you are Shane, right? how are you? you don't mind doing this job, right?".* Shane answers, *"I am good."* Mitchie wonders, *'he sounds so cold and distant... have I said something wrong?'.* Joanna says, *"since we are all set, I will go to the hospital administration to complete your discharge, you two can get to know each other better, ok?".* Joanna leaves the room as Mitchie thinks, *'he's shy maybe because someone else was here, since we are alone I could get some more information about him... he's such a cute and sexy bodyguard... teasing him sounds like fun too, perhaps I can open the conversation again!'.* Mitchie says, *"ok, Shane let's talk, we will have a conversation like a normal human, ok?".* Shanc looks at her as Mitchie asks, *"first question, how long have you been a bodyguard?".*

Shane replies, *"five years."* Mitchie ponders, *'I want to know more about intimate things....'* Mitchie boldly says, *"are you single?."* Shane is stunned by her question answering, *"what?."* Mitchie curiously says, *"because I would like to know."* Shane says, *"it is not important for the job."*

Mitchie wonders, *'huh? I am so curious now, because, why not?'.* Mitchie playfully bats her eyes saying, *"perhaps a little affair with a celebrity you worked with before, tell me! tell me, spill everything to me".* Shane notices her teasing but firmly says, *"no, I am very professional with my job, got it?".* Mitchie plays her fingers in her hair saying, *"are you sure? I am open minded and can keep a secret... with a look like you've got, you cannot be single".* She giggles as Shane rolls his eyes asking, *"are you always like this?".* Mitchie replies, *"you will get to know me more later".* Shane sighs saying, *"I already regret this."* Mitchie asks, *"do you remember me?."* Shane answers, *"of course, I do."* Mitchie says, *"hmmm, is there anything you would like to ask me?".* Shane replies, *"not really."*

Mitchie was surprised saying, *"but, you should ask me something! I am basically talking to myself here."* Shane says, *"fine, I will ask you something... how are you feeling? Are you ok?."* Mitchie replies, *"I am ok."* Shane asks, *"are you hungry?."* Mitchie nods saying, *"I am! see it's not that hard to engage in a conversation".* Shane says, *"you see, I would prefer to keep everything professional, we don't need to build a friendship or something more... it will be strictly professional between you and me so you don't need to try to engage in a conversation with me, I will still do my job perfectly".* Mitchie giggles as Shane asks, *"why are you laughing?".* Mitchie answers, *"I have never come across or met someone as cold as you, but still, I would like to be your friend... you look like the lonely type, I will be your first friend then".* She gets up from the bed as Shane asks, *"are you okay standing up like that?".* Mitchie replies, *"I am fine."* He comes closer to her asking, *"where is your phone?."* Mitchie quickly replies, *"It's in here with me, why? are we going to exchange numbers?".* Shane holds out his hand saying, *"your phone, please".* Mitchie opens the drawer and hands it over to him as he quickly does something before giving it back to her; Mitchie asks, *"what did you do?".* Shane replies, *"I set a GPS in your phone, that way I can easily track you".* Mitchie says, *"but, can I still have your phone number? it's normal to have each other's phone number, right?."* Shane says, *"I have already put my number in your phone too".*

Mitchie says, *"really? that's great! Now, you have to save my number."* Shane says, *"I already have your number, your brother Darren gave me your number before".* Mitchie says, *"oh that's splendid."* Just then Joanna comes back saying, *"I have handled the admiration and your discharge documents, we are good to go".* Mitchie says, *"yay! Let me clean up and change my clothes".*

Chapter 6

Mitchie grabs her clothes from the chair and goes into the bathroom; she looks in the mirror thinking, *'finally I can change into my pretty clothes'.* She removes the hospital gown and wears a mini-skirt and black top. She brushes her hair before washing her face and doing her makeup. She comes out of the room just as Joanna says, *"Mitchie, we have a bad situation right now...".* Mitchie asks, *"what is wrong, Jo?".* Joanna replies, *"the media... the reporter and press are outside waiting for you".* Mitchie was stunned saying, *"what?! how?! W-what are we going to do now?".* Shane replies, *"no worries, Mitchie I could help you avoid them by using the back door, it's my duty to keep you safe, I will try my best as it's my first mission, just take my hand and trust me".* He extends his hand to her as she thinks, *'ugh, I really don't want to deal and face the reporters....'.* She takes Shane's hand saying, *"let's use the back door to escape".* Shane says, *"good, I prefer the back door too",* Joanna says, *"I will face and deal the reporters and press at the front door since they have already seen me".* Mitchie looks at Joanna saying, *"good luck, Jo".* Shane and Mitchie run out to the corridor as she stops asking, *"ugh, why can't reporters just leave me alone?".* Shane replies, *"because you are a celebrity, thank you for wanting to use the back door, less work for me".* Mitchie says, *"you are so lazy! I cannot believe you want less work; I should have just faced the reporters and press instead!".*

Shane says, *"hey, every bodyguard never likes crowded places, we prefer, we also prefer the safest road, of course... it's normal".* Mitchie giggles saying, *"let's go".* They head out from the fire exit just as one of the reporters says, *"MITCHIE TORRES IS IN THE HOSPITAL!"*. Mitchie panics as Shane holds her against the wall saying, *"stand still"*. He comes closer to her lips as the reporters pass them while Mitchie notice Shane's face close to her saying, *"Shane... umm.... I think it's safe now..."*. Shane moves back saying, *"sorry"*. Mitchie giggles seeing this and teases him playfully saying, *"keeping it all professional, hm?"*. Shane says stunned, *"what are you talking about? I was covering you so no one could spot you, I only did my job"*. Mitchie comes over and kisses Shane's cheek saying, *"sure..."* She giggles at him while he blushes and looks a little annoyed; Mitchie sees Shane's cheek go red saying, *"aww, you are so cute... you are blushing"*. Shane rolls his eyes saying, *"I am not, what is wrong with doing my job? This is nonsense"*. Mitchie smiles saying, *"relax, I was just teasing you... you are so rigid, it's adorable"*. Shane sighs again saying, *"you are unbelievable"*. Mitchie winks playfully at him as he says, *"come on let's go before someone comes back"*. Soon in the car Shane was driving however said, *"from now on, I will drive you anywhere you go"*.

Mitchie thinks, *'he will drive me anywhere....'* Mitchie replies, *"yes, sir!"*. Shane says, *"now we will head back to your place"*. Mitchie opens the door saying, *"home sweet home!"*. Shane looks around saying, *"cool place you have"*. Someone barks at him as Mitchie turns and bends down to see her brown and white corgi looking at her; Mitchie rubs his tummy saying, *"Mocco I missed you"*. Shane says, *"you have a dog?"*. Mocco barks at him before coming over and sniffing his hand; Mitchie watches Shane bend over and rub Mocco's ear saying, *"I think he likes you... his name is Mocco"*. Shane says, *"I think I like him too...."*. Mitchie says, *"you can leave now and come back tomorrow morning"*. Shane says, *"you are absurd, I will be staying here from now on"*. Mitchie was stunned saying, *"WHAT?! you are going to live with me?!"*. Shane says, *"that's what I just said"*. Mitchie says, *"o....okay! I heard you, ok?"*. Shane asks, *"then why do you look so stunned and surprised?"*. Mitchie replies, *"because I never had someone in my apartment"*. Mocco barks at her as Mitchie says, *"I meant a real person and I am actually happy to hear that, now I have another friend to talk to! Someone to play games, have dinner and talk to".* Mocco whines sadly as Mitchie lifts him in her arms saying, *"I love you Mocco but not in that way".* Shane says, *"I did not expect this kind of reaction from you Ms Mitchie".* Mitchie looks at Shane saying, *"hm, what sort of reaction were you expecting from me?".* Shane says, *"shocked? Stunned? Denial? everyone is like that, no one really likes to share their home with a complete stranger".* Mitchie giggles saying, *"silly, I am not like any other girls, and I enjoy having a company".*

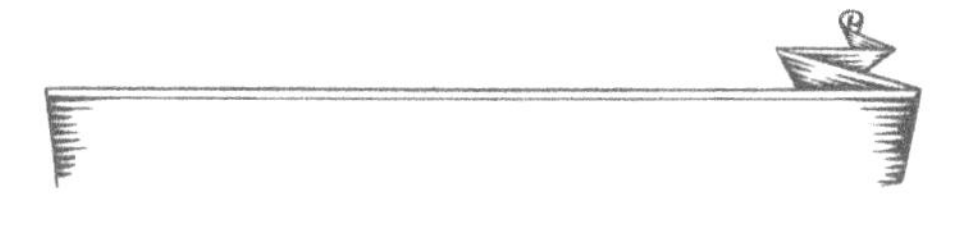

Chapter 7

Mitchie says, *"you can take the guest room, let me show you!."* Shane follows Mitchie to another room saying, *"here is the guest room, you can use it".* He looks around saying, *"it looks cozy, thanks".* Mitchie says, *"and there's one bathroom in this apartment so we will have to share it".* Shane says, *"sounds good to me."* Mitchie says, *"I am going to use the bathroom first, ok?"* Shane says, *"ok."* Mocco climbs on the bed and curls himself into a ball while Mitchie is just about to head out before saying, *"If you need anything at all, call me".* Soon Mitchie comes to her room grabbing her towel and heads into the shower; she lets the hot water wash her body singing, *"I wish I could forever hold you in my arms... I will love you forever...wherever... we're mean to be together".* Mitchie wonders, *'a little sad song sounds great for my single or album.... I wonder if Jo would approve of it...'.* She continues to be lost in her thoughts when there is a knock on the door; Shane says, "Mitchie, are you alright in there? I heard something from the bathroom." Mitchie replies, *"of course I am ok! I was singing!"* Shane asks, *"are you sure about that? I thought I heard a scream."* Mitchie replies, *"no, Shane! Now leave me in peace, you will have your turn to use the bathroom later!".* Shane rolls his eyes saying, *"I will be waiting for you in the living room".*

Mitchie says, *"ok."* She turns to head back to the shower however slips on a soap and falls screaming, *"AAAAHHHH!!."* Shane is stunned to hear her scream saying, *"MITCHIE! I am coming in."* He opens the door looking around saying, *"Mitchie, are you ok?"* Mitchie is faced on the floor saying, *"ow...."* Shane sees her saying, *"Mitchie, I hope you are not hurt, here take my hand... let me help you".* Mitchie looks up at Shane extending her hand saying, *"yes, help me.... Please, but I need my towel...."* Shane drops it on her face as she says, *"ugh, why my face?".* Shane says, *"I am trying not to look at your naked body, ok? Use the towel to cover your body and I will help you".* He turns around as Mitchie slowly gets up and wraps the towel around her body saying, *"ugh.....".* Shane turns around seeing Mitchie covered and lifts her in his arms; she nervously says, *"this is a little embarrassing....."* Shane says, *"it's for your safety."* He brings to her bedroom saying, *"I will put you down now".* He lays her on the bed asking, *"how are you feeling now?".* Mitchie replies, *"I am feeling better now, thank you... having a bodyguard is not so bad".* Shane rolls his eyes saying, *"I will be just outside".* Just as he is about to leave Mitchie says, *"wait!".* She thinks, *'I cannot just let him go! I need to do something!'* She comes over and kisses Shane's cheek leaving him stunned and surprised. Shane asks, *"what was that for?."* Mitchie replies, *"it's a thank you, kiss".* Shane says, *"you don't have to do that".* Mitchie says, *"it is just a kiss, now shoo shoo."*

Shane says, *"if you need anything, just call me".* Mitchie says, *"ditto."* Shane leaves as Mitchie grabs her PJs and sighs before soon heading over to the living room and asking, *"have you settled in, Shane?."* Shane was sitting on the couch with Mocco beside him replying, *"yes, I am all good".* Mitchie stomach growls as she says, *"I must be hungry".* Shane asks, *"do you have any food?".* Mitchie replies, *"I am not sure.... but."* She goes over to the piano and sits down singing, *"tell me why I am waiting for you.... I am hungry so hungry... please feeed me.... Sushi, chicken, and noodles are all my favorites".* Shane thought, *'she is one bizarre girl....'* He gets up saying, *"show me to your kitchen."* Mitchie says, *"aww, but I still want to play the piano".* Shane sighs saying, *"come on."* Mitchie gets up saying, *"ok, here I come."* Shane thinks to himself, *'she's bizarre but cute.'* Soon in the kitchen Shane had a look through the fridge and cupboard only to find a few dog food packs and treats. Shane says, *"you don't have anything in your kitchen, Mitchie... how come? How do you survive?*

I can cook for you if you want." Mitchie was surprised thinking, *'omg, he's going to cook for me....'* Mitchie excitedly says, *"I would love to eat your food! It must be delicious... guys who cook are amazing".* She winks playfully at him as he says, *"I am going to go shopping".* Mitchie says, *"ok, I will wait at home with Mocco".* Shane says, *"make sure to lock the door."* Mitchie nods while Shane continues saying, *"if something happens, call me".* Mitchie teases him saying, *"so possessive."* Shane rolls his eyes and says, *"bye"* before leaving.

Chapter 8

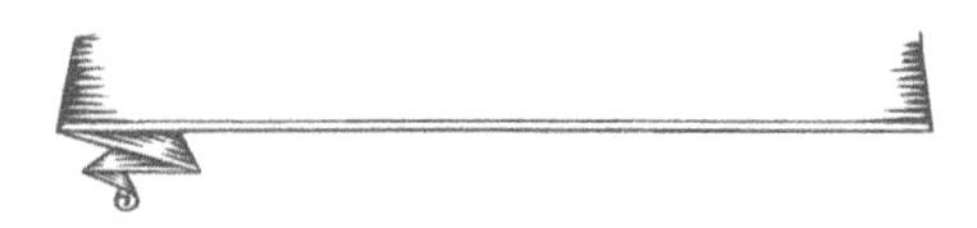

Mitchie ponders for a few moments before heading back to the piano and sees Mocco sleeping beside her. She plays a few notes singing, *"Heart and soul, I fell in love with you...."* A few hours pass as she yawns feeling sleepy and decides to text Shane; she texts, *'Shane, where are you?'.* Shane texts back, 'on my way home, the store is quite crowded at night, many sales, and customers'. Mitchie texts, *'are you still at the store?'. Shane texts back, 'no, I'm on my way back home, I told you, I need to focus... stop texting me'.* Mitchie texts, *'but you still are replying...'.* Shane texts, *'because you keep texting me'.* Mitchie texts, *'I like talking with you, I want to talk to you....'.* Shane texts, *'the more you text me, the slower I am going to be back to the apartment'.* Mitchie texts, *'I miss you, come back home soon!* Shane texts, *'what?'.* Mitchie texts, *'I miss having you around the apartment, I know I have Mocco but he's a sleepy bug...'.* Shane texts, *'are you ok? Any emergencies?'.* Mitchie texts, *'don't you miss me? talking with me?'.* Shane texts, *'maybe... I will be home soon'.* Mitchie texts, *'okay!'.* She yawns thinking, *'I will wait for Shane in my bed'.* She carries Mocco to her room and places him on the bed as she lays closing her eyes saying, *"I will sleep for a few minutes".* A few moments later there is a loud crash noise as Mitchie wakes up wondering, *'huh? what was that sound?'.* She comes out to check as she sees a hooded figure and grabs her baseball bat; she hits the unknown figure asking, *"WHO ARE YOU?!".* Shane drops the bag and grabs his arm saying, *"ow! Ouch!".*

Mitchie sees Shane saying, *"Shane? oh my god, I am so sorry! I-I didn't know it was you!"*. Shane says, *"really?"*. Mitchie again apologises asking, *"are you o-okay?"*. Shane rolls his eyes replying, *"do I look like I am okay?"*. Mitchie had an idea as she said sadly, *"I am so sorry"*. She comes over and kisses Shane's cheek leaving him surprised; she smiles saying, *"I kissed the pain away"*. Shane asks stunned, *"why did you do that?"*. Mitchie answers, *"I told you that I kissed the pain away"*. Shane rolls his eyes saying, *"you are uncontrollable, wild and untamed… like an animal"*. Mitchie giggles while he says, *"remember Mitchie, this is a professional work, you don't kiss your bodyguard"*. Mitchie says, *"but, I just feel guilty that I hurt you, it's an apology kiss but also to make your pain go away"*. Shane rolls his eyes saying, *"I am not a baby, I do not need a kiss to make the pain go away and it doesn't hurt that much"*. Mitchie says, *"you are cold yet so interesting, it's so much fun talking to you"*.

Shane says, *"anyway I got dinner for us"*. They head to the kitchen as Shane serves up the chicken pot pie with mash potato and cream horseradish sauce; Mitchie was impressed by the food saying, *"yum! The food's aroma smells delicious"*. They both eat and enjoy it as after Mitchie thanks Shane for the meal. Shane asks, *"can I ask you a question?"*. Mitchie looks at him replying, *"what is it?"*. Shane says, *"you were singing something in the bathroom, right? I have never heard that song before"*. Mitchie says, *"you said I was screaming! I told you that I was ok…"*. Shane says, *"well I am curious now…"*. Mitchie wonders, *'he's interested in my song…..'* Mitchie gets up singing the lyrics before soon asking, *"so Shane, how was I? what do you think?"*. Shane replies, *"sounds like a platonic love story but nice"*. Mitchie says, *"It's supposed to be a sad song"*. Shane asks, *"then? Why don't you release the song?"*. Mitchie nervously replies, *"I-I don't know if anyone will enjoy a sad song by me, I don't know if Joanna or the producer will like it"*. Shane says, *"you will never know until you try"*. Mitchie asks, *"but do you like the song? I am not sure if it's a good song or not"*. Shane says, *"it's a good song and it will be a surprise to your fans since you have never sung a sad song before which is a good thing"*. Mitchie says, *"wow, you sound like the perfect manager"*. Shane rolls his eyes saying, *"it's just my opinion"*. Mitchie thanks him before he gets up and goes over to the sink saying, *"I will wash the dishes and you can go to rest"*. Mitchie asks, *"are you sure? I can assist you with cleaning the dishes!"*. Shane says, *"no it's fine, get some rest"*. Mitchie nods and says, *"Good night"* before heading back to her room. She climbs into her bed and is about to fall asleep when her phone beeps she sees a text from an unknown number which says, *'Hello, Mitchie. This is not over yet... prepare for the worst'*. Mitchie deletes the text and takes a deep breath before falling asleep. The next day, Mitchie wakes up to see Shane in the kitchen preparing her breakfast as she says, *"Good morning Shane"*. Shane replies, *"morning Mitchie, how are you feeling?"*.

Mitchie sighs saying, *"so tired, I wish I had the day off"*. Just then Joanna comes in saying, *"morning everyone, last night me and the producer decided to make a statement post about the explosion incident as well as an apology to the victims that were affected... no bad comments so far, and everyone is so supportive, and we are planning to have a makeup concert with some other artists too!"*. Mitchie smiles saying, *"god, what would I do without you, Jo? You are simply an amazing person!"*. Joanna says, *"now, we have a photoshoot for your deluxe album today, I've prepared your dresses"*. Joanna hands her a bag as Mitchie thanks her and heads to her room to get dressed. After trying a few options Mitchie chooses a light pink dress as she styles her hair and makeup before came downstairs saying, *"I'm ready"*. Joanna says, *"ok, let's go"*. They soon head over the photoshoot as the photographer says, *"alright Mitchie, give me a smile"*. Mitchie does a few poses as Shane thinks, *'cute.....'* He takes his phone and captures her photo thinking, *'I guess it's ok to keep a picture of her, she is so cute'*. Shane smiles to himself; soon after in the dressing room Joanna gave Mitchie a giftbag saying, *"Mitchie, there's a gift for you from your fan, by the way great photoshoot today!"*. Joanna leaves Mitchie to get some rest as Mitchie opens the giftbag and screams in shock seeing a spoiled rotten smelly meat. Her phone beeps as she sees a text from the unknown person, *'hello, Mitchie... do you like my gift? A spoiled meat, hm? this spoiled meat indicates what you will be when I finally get you'.* Mitchie panics thinking, *'no, I need to find Shane!'.*

Chapter 9

She comes out of the room seeing a crowd of reporters around Joanna; one of them says, *"we need to speak with Mitchie!"*. Joanna says, *"no, Mitchie is busy, what do you want to ask her?"*. The reporter replies. *"we would like to ask her about the explosion's connection to Kaitlyn Torres's unsolved murder mystery"*. Joanna says, *"please leave Mitchie alone, I request all of you to go home."* Mitchie thinks, *'oh no... I should leave....'* Just then someone spots her saying, *"that's Mitchie!."* The reporters attempt to crowd around Mitchie however Joanna comes in front of her; the reporter says, *"Mitchie, can I have a minute of your time? I promise it will be quick."* Joanna says, *"please, Mitchie is busy."* Another reporter says, *"but you can give us a statement, Mitchie? Just anything, otherwise we cannot promise what you will see on tomorrow's newspaper"*. Mitchie is stunned wondering, *'are they threatening me? I need to stay calm and maintain a good image'.* She says, *"I would like everyone not to mention my mother, please... she is at peace now, so please let her be and about the accident, I am glad that everyone is safe and ok however I cannot help that I feel a little guilty and sad about it, but I believe this has nothing to do with my mother's case so please leave my mother alone."* A reporter asks, *"what about the explosion? Do you know something about it, Mitchie?."*

Mitchie replies, *"no comment, I'm sorry but I have to go now"*. The reporter says, *"no, Mitchie! We have a few more questions!."* Mitchie apologises and turns just as Shane runs over to her saying, *"Mitchie, I've got you"*. Mitchie says, *"take me out from here, I can't deal with this"*.

Shane whispers, *"when I say run, you run".* Mitchie nods as he tells her to run, and they both escape as the reporters try to call out to her. Soon they head down the corridor as Mitchie asks, *"where should we go?!."* Shane replies, *"let's hide in a room."* They soon hide in a storage room as Shane asks, *"Mitchie, are you ok?".* Mitchie replies, *"not really, how about you.... Are you ok, Shane?."* Shane nods saying, *"I am ok, we can hide here for a while, I think".* Mitchie sighs saying, *"yeah, I don't like the press... it's better here".* They look at each other before Shane says, *"want to talk about it?".* Mitchie says, *"about what?."* Shane says, *"your mother? I don't want to force you to tell me if you are uncomfortable, I just thought maybe you needed to let your feelings out of your chest."* Mitchie says, *"let me tell you about her story.... You see, my mom was a singer; she didn't know that there was an unknown person stalking her".* Shane asks, *"why did she not know that?".* Mitchie replies, *"because she could never think of anything like that, my grandpa always told me that she cared about everyone and always assumed everyone was good and kind... my mom should have known that not all people are that good, she was even nice to her haters".*

Shane asks, *"why? Did she refuse to see the worst in people?."* Mitchie replies, *"I think so, she was just too good to people that doesn't imply that she was dumb or stupid, ok? I just wish the media would stop asking questions about my mother... she is at peace now... no one ever talked about this issue until the explosion happened".* Shane says, *"let's not talk about it then, we should focus on how to get out of this place".* Mitchie says, *"I will call Darren and make him help us out! The reporters are also interested with him, not just me."* Shane says, *"good idea, we need that! This might be our way to escape from here."* Mitchie takes out her phone texting Darren, *'Darren, are you there? I need your help!.'* Darren texted back, *'Mitchie! For you, sis? Always, tell me?.'* Mitchie texts, *'reporters are in my photoshoot studio, I am stuck!.'* Darren texts, *'I am coming to help, don't worry'.* Mitchie texts, *'thank you... you are the best, you know that?!'.* Darren texts, *'I know.'* Mitchie puts her phone away telling Shane with a smile, *"he is coming to help!."* Shane says, *"that's great news!."* A few moments later Darren came asking, *"who wants my autograph?!."* The film crew assistant was behind him saying, *"not again! Mr Torres! You cannot keep running away from the set!."* The reporters spot him as one yells, *"THAT'S DARREN TORRES!".* Darren blows a kiss saying, *"come and get me!".* He runs as the reporters chase him along with the film crew; A few moments pass as Mitchie gets a text from Darren confirming the coast is clear to escape. They come out of the closet as Shane says, *"I have to admit, your brother is very reliable!".* Mitchie says, *"he is!."* Shane asks, *"are you reliable too, Mitchie?."*

Chapter 10

Mitchie looks at Shane replying, *"hey, I am very reliable!"*. Shane laughs saying, *"we should go before they come back."* He heads out while Mitchie calls out, *"wait!"* She finally comes out of the building and into Shane's car as she says, *"finally we are in the car safely"*. Shane asks, *"how are you feeling? Are we good to go?"* Mitchie replies, *"we are good to go however let's stop at my favorite restaurant, food is my love language... dinner is very important!."* Shane says, *"whatever you want, Mitchie... so tell me your food order?"*. They drive to the restaurant carpark as Mitchie says, *"hey! I am coming to the restaurant with you"*. Shane says, *"absolutely no way, just tell me your order"*. Mitchie firmly says, *"I am coming with you and that's final! You can't stop me."* They soon head inside as a woman sees Mitchie saying, *"Mitchie! The usual?"* Mitchie says, *"Hi Jane, the usual please and a sirloin steak for my bodyguard"*. Jane nods and says, *"ok, wait here"*. Shane asks, *"you know the owner?"*. Mitchie replies, *"I told you that I am going to order my own food, you will not understand my order"*. Three girls spot Mitchie as Nadira says, *"omg that's Mitchie!"*. Mitchie looks at the girls as Shane comes in front of her with a cold firm look; the girls look away intimated as Holly says, *"her bodyguard is so scary"*. Mitchie whispers to him, *"Shane, you are scaring them!"*. Shane turns to her saying, *"it's for your safety"*. Mitchie says, *"they are normal people, Shane"*. Shane says, *"you have to be cautious"*. Mitchie says, *"not with my fans! they look so nervous, I really want to talk to them"*. She pleads, *"please Shane, let me talk to my fans... you can still watch over me!"*. Shane says, *"fine, but be*

quick". Mitchie comes over as the girls smile seeing her; she says, *"hello, how are you all doing? Sorry about my bodyguard, we are on guard these days".*

Bella says, "no, Mitchie! We are so happy *to see you here!"* Holly says, *"thank you for approaching us!".* Nadira says, *"we were scared to approach you but here you are... you are so kind".* Holly asks, *"are you ok, Mitchie?".* Bella says, *"we were so worried because of the explosion, you know....".* Mitchie says, *"thank you so much but I am fine."* Shane soon calls out to her, *"Mitchie!."* Mitchie says, *"ah, sorry I have to go now".* Bella asks, *"wait, can we take a picture together, Mitchie?".* Mitchie replies, *"sure, of course."* They pose as one of the girls captures the selfie; Mitchie says, *"I have to go now, thank you everyone."* The girls thank Mitchie who goes over to her table to have dinner with Shane. Soon after dinner they come out to the carpark where they both see an unknown guy doing something to the car. Mitchie sees the hooded figure saying, *"OMG! Shane, look at that!"* Shane has an angry expression as Mitchie says, *"OMG! We must catch him!"*

Shane tells her to wait before slowly sneaking quietly and pinning down the guy to the ground. Mitchie says, *"OMG! I-is it all over?"* A few moments later in the police station one of the officers says, *"sorry to inform you this but the guy is not who we are looking for".* Alex says, *"I swear I didn't mean to do anything weird; I was trying to sneak a gift into the car for Mitchie!".* The officer says, *"It's still a crime for trying to get into someone's car without permission".* Shane asks, *"what do you think, Mitchie?".* Mitchie wonders, *'he is innocent... he has good intentions to me, I don't want to complicate this.'* Mitchie says, *"I would like him to be free, he has good intentions so it's ok".* Shane asks, *"are you sure about this?".* Mitchie nods saying, *"yes, no one got hurt and it was just a big misunderstanding".* Alex says, *"so I am free?."* Mitchie says, *"of course."* Alex says, *"ah, Mitchie is truly kind like everyone said, thank you so much lovely Mitchie... but will you accept my gift? It's a bunch of flowers... your favorite white roses."* Mitchie gets up taking the gift saying, *"thank you so much".* Alex leaves while Shane says, *"shall we go now?".* Mitchie nods as she thanks Alex again before he leaves. Soon Shane and Mitchie come home as Mitchie comes over to Mocco and wakes him up to feed him. Soon in the living room Mitchie says, *"what a day, huh?."* Shane asks, *"did you not have fun, today? We survived today."* Mitchie smiles saying, *"thanks to you! Thank you for taking care of me."* Shane says, *"it's my job".* Mitchie's phone beeps as she sees a message come in; Mitchie says, *"it's a text from Joanna".* Shane notices Mitchie's worried expression asking, *"what's wrong, Mitchie?".*

Chapter 11

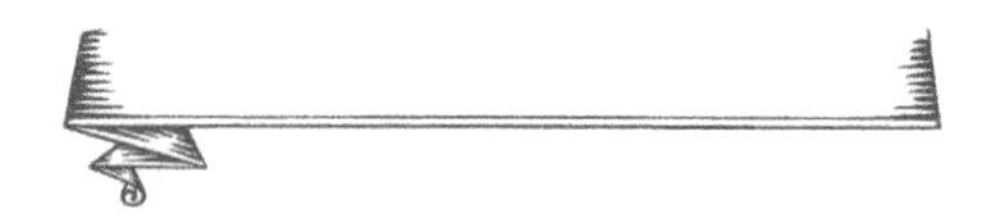

Mitchie sighs replying, *"Joanna said people in the social media are talking about my mother's murder case again, she sent me the video link".* Shane says, *"check it if you want, it will make you feel better".* Mitchie nods and clicks on the link as a tiktok video appears with someone saying, *"so, guys! I believe the explosion at Mitchie Torres's concert is connected to Kaitlyn Torres's unsolved murder case, why did I say this? because Mitchie Torres is a good person and I don't think she has any enemies... her one and only enemy is her mother's murderer, right? Does this mean the old unsolved murder case of Kaitlyn Torres will be reopened? Will the police investigate this case further now? let me know what you guys think!."* Mitchie sighs saying, *"nothing serious but... I think people will be suspicious about this incident and will not leave it alone".* Shane asks, *"do you agree with what she said?".* Mitchie replies, *"I don't know...."* Shane says, *"hey that's ok, it is nothing serious... people can say anything they want and whatever they want about you and your mother's case, but you don't need to worry or think about that, it has not harmed your reputation or career".* Mitchie says, *"you are right, Shane... I was just nervous about it...."* Shane says, *"Mitchie you will be fine, I've got you, ok?".* Mitchie says, *"ok but the fact the police have not made any progress on this stalker makes me feel nervous and I am anxious about it...I also feel uneasy".* Shane says, *"Mitchie, I promise you that I will protect you until this problem is solved, do you hear me?".* Mitchie replies, *"thank you, Shane, you are so kind".* Shane says, *"I am just worried about your health, ok?".*

Mitchie has an idea as she says, *"sit Shane, I am going to perform something special".* Mitchie plays a few note and sings, *'with you I feel safe, so loved and protected..'.* After playing Shane says, *"that's a good song."* Mitchie says, *"you think so? The lyrics sounds a little mellow and not very innocent".* Shane asks, *"does that matter?."* Mitchie replies, *"perhaps I think too much... I shouldn't, right?."* Shane says, *"you shouldn't, you know that you have a very special beautiful voice and I think you are the only singer who can touch someone's heart... I mean look at your fans, they adore and love you... a little sad song will only make your fans love you even more".*

Mitchie gets up saying, *"look at you, you said something so sweet and nice to me, I never knew you felt that way about my music and voice... no one has ever very directly told me this".* Shane says, *"I only said the truth, that is all".* Mitchie asks, *"are you in love with me or something?."* Shane is taken aback saying stunned, *"what?! no!".* Mitchie has a playful smirk asking, *"are you sure? That's ok, it's not the first time I have received love confession".* Shane says, *"you are an amazing singer, that's all... atleast that is how I feel, are you teasing me, Mitchie? That is not cool, ok?."* Mitchie says, *"teasing? I don't know what you mean... are you enjoying yourself? We are totally flirting at each other, aren't we?."* Shane coldly replies, *"no."* Mitchie says, *"you are adorable".* Shane says, *"thanks."* Mitchie says, *"don't be cold to me, you like me... you are blushing".* Shane says, *"no way!."* Mitchie giggles thinking, *'he is so cute, w-wait what is this feeling? I've never felt this way towards someone before.... but him.'* Mitchie says, *"you are a good person, Shane and you told me to keep everything professional, but our relationship grows".* Shane says, *"to be honest, I didn't expect you to act the same way on and off camera, most people that I have worked with are quite different from who they are on TV, they can act all nice and sweet in front of the camera however turn ugly when the camera is turned off... you are just being who you are in front and behind the camera.... I feel comfortable with you."* Mitchie comes over saying, *"that is so sweet, I feel comfortable with you too*". Shane says, "*yeah?.*" She comes over and sits on his lap saying, "*yes that's why I.... I like you a lot.*" They stare into each other's eyes for a moment before Mitchie kisses Shane.

Chapter 12

Mitchie and Shane are still kissing and in every moment they feel it deepening; Mitchie thinks, *'Shane kissed me back! this is like a dream! I can't help that I want to kiss him more, he tastes so sweet, and I love kissing him already'.* Shane says, *"Mitchie... we have to stop."* Mitchie says, *"but, you taste so good, I can't stop now."* Shane says, *"if we don't stop now...."* Mitchie asks, *"if we don't stop now?."* Shane replies, *"I don't think I can control myself anymore...."* Mitchie says, *"then, don't."* Shane says, *"I can't."* He pulls himself back saying, *"I am sorry, Mitchie but I think it's best if we keep our relationship professional".* Mitchie says, *"no...."* Shane says, *"Mitchie, we can't I am your bodyguard, let's just keep it that way, let's forget what just happened, ok?".* He apologises again before getting up and heading to his room. Mitchie looks sadly thinking, *'this is stupid.'* The next day Mitchie is in her room choosing what to wear for her the TV show interview; Mitchie eventually chooses a blue dress and heads to the studio with Shane; Joanna sees her and brings her to the makeup room to get her ready as Joanna checks the schedule saying, *"five minutes left, I will check if everything is good".* Mitchie comes out and sees Shane wondering, *'should I go over and talk to him?'.* Mitchie asks, "*why are you standing so far from me, Shane?".* Shane replies, *"no, why would I do that?".* Mitchie says, *"you are".* Shane looks at her asking, *"do you want to talk?".* Mitchie nods replying, *"sure, let's talk so, about last night...".* Shane says, *"you know, we should forget about it, to keep things professional and easier, we should forget it ever happened".* Mitchie says, *"but, it happened... it happened,*

ok?". Shane says, *"that's why I told you that we should forget about it".* Mitchie says, *"you can't tell me what to do, you are not my mom".* Shane rolls his eyes asking, *"why are you so stubborn?".* Mitchie replies, *"it's not my fault that you kissed me back, don't hate the fact that we kissed".*

Shane says, *"it's useless to reason with you, you will not listen anyway".* Mitchie says, *"you are trying to tell me what do, it's my life, so you can't tell me what to do".* Shane rolls his eyes saying, *"fine, whatever you want".* Mitchie senses Shane's annoyance asking, *"did I get on your nerve?".* Shane replies, *"always."* Mitchie winks playfully saying, "and I love getting into your nerves". Shane says, *"you are terrible."* Mitchie winks again saying, *"you are welcome."* Soon Mitchie is doing a rehearsal singing, *'you me, every touch makes me wanna give you my heart, the melody to my music'.* Later that afternoon Mitchie has a TV interview with Isaac who says, *"Mitchie Torres, how have you been?".* Mitchie replies, *"good, how about you?."* Isaac answers, *"I am very well, thank you; it's been a while since you were here, would you like to tell me what were you doing after the terrible incident? I hope you are okay talking about it."* Mitchie replies, *"of course Isaac, I am so grateful and happy that all of my fans give me a lot of support".* After a few hours Mitchie thought, *'ugh I wish this interview ends quickly.....'* Later in the makeup room Shane asks, *"do you want to go home now? we should go straight home, it's not safe anywhere".* Mitchie says, *"oh yeah, take me home... talk shows are such a misery for an introvert like me".* Shane says, *"you? an introvert? I doubt that."* Mitchie says, *"I am actually an introvert."* Shane says, *"cool."* Just then the door opens as a young woman comes in saying, *"Mitchie Torres in the flesh! Don't you remember me?."* Mitchie gets up saying, *"Nala! of course, I remember you, aren't you supposed to be in Milan?".* Nala replies, *"well, I have a little shooting break, it's been a while and I want to support my bestie in her misery".* Shane says, *"I will leave you two alone."* He leaves as Nala comes over saying, *"so? Who is that hottie?."* Mitchie replies, *"Shane is my bodyguard."* Nala says, *"you lucky girl! so? While I am here, do you want to go out with me? I am bored and lonely, and I missed you so much and I care about you, and...and....*" Mitchie says, "*I would love to hang out, but you see... I don't think my bodyguard will be happy with that*". Nala says, "*you haven't even asked him yet*". Soon Mitchie goes to speak with Shane who says, "*no!*". Mitchie says, "*girls just wanna have fun! You will be there so it will be fine.*" Shane firmly says, "*no means no.*" Mitchie uses her charm saying, "*I will kiss you if you let me go and have fun, deal?.*" She winks playfully at him as Shane blushes deeply while Mitchie says, "*I'll take that as a yes*".

Chapter 13

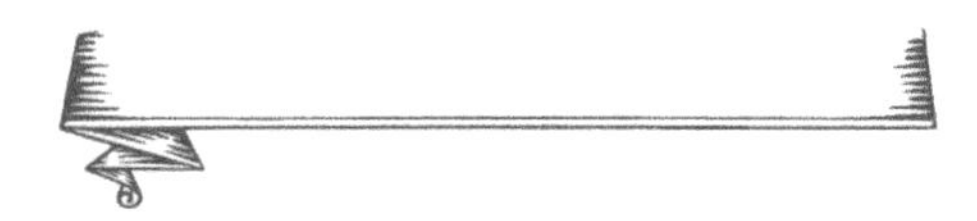

Mitchie comes back to the room and heads into the bathroom to change her outfit; she comes back in an emerald green dress. Soon at the club Nala says, *"it's been a while since we had this much fun!"*. Mitchie replies, *"yeah, especially after all of the incidents, I am so glad you are here!"*. They both dance to the music before Mitchie soon feels parched as Nala says, *"ask your bodyguard to get a drink for you"*. Mitchie turns to see Shane drinking a can of soda before soon leaving. Mitchie says, *"oh, he is leaving."* Nala suddenly spots someone saying, *"Mitchie! Danger!."* The person is a young woman asking two other girls to be her in her murder mystery vlog. The woman soon sees Mitchie saying, *"Mitchie Torres in the flesh!"*. Mitchie looks panickily at Nala who says, *"she is that famous murder mystery vlogger, right?!"*. Mitchie says, *"I am going!."* She runs away as the woman comes over as Nala says, *"hold it right there! interview me, talk to me the one and only Nala Vancouver"*. She runs out down a corridor near the fire escape to catch her breath thinking, *'safe! I should go look for Shane.'* Just then an unknown figure comes behind her grabbing her arm as Mitchie turns and punches the person. She stops saying, *"Shane!."* Shane asks, *"what are you doing here, Mitchie? You should not be walking alone; you could be in danger... you are lucky that I saw you leave"*. Mitchie says, *"hey, I can take care of myself, I can protect myself"*. Shane looks at her saying, *"are you sure about that, Mitchie?"*. Mitchie replies, *"I learned karate when I was in primary school!."* Shane says, *"of course you did"*. Mitchie senses the sarcasm in his tone replying, *"you don't believe me, do you?!"*.

Shane replies, *"no, if you could take care of yourself, your brother would not have hired me".* Mitchie rolls her eyes saying, *"he is just overprotective of me".* Shane asks, *"can you stop being so stubborn for a moment? What's your problem?."* Mitchie answers, *"my problem is you; you drive me crazy".* Shane says stunned, *"what? what did I do?".* Mitchie says, *"I'm annoyed, ok?! one day you acted like you cared about me and the next day you acted differently towards me and then we kissed... and I love it, and then you want me to forget everything, as if it never happened".* She sighs before saying, *"I don't know if you are playing with my feelings or if I am exaggerating everything... sorry".* Shane says, *"Mitchie, you do not understand this situation, I am your bodyguard and it's better if we keep everything professional, it's easier for my job and yours too... do you understand?".* Mitchie answers, *"I....I don't know."* Shane says, *"Mitchie, look.... it's not like I don't want anything with you, it's just I.... I like being with you but I......"* Mitchie says, *"but, you.....? no, I don't understand because I know you want me too, we can have something not professional and it's ok, don't you want something with me? what do you think about me?".* Shane replies, *"I think you are.... sweet and kind, it is impossible for anyone not to like you, but Mitchie.... don't be selfish, ok?."* Mitchie asks, *"then why did you kiss me back?."* Shane answers, *"I guess, I got carried away."* Mitchie says, *"or simply, you like me too and it's ok, you know that I care about you, right? I simply don't like this 'professional' relationship thing, if we can be friends then we can be something more too."* Shane comes over and kisses her unexpectedly as she closes her eyes kissing him deeper saying, *"I knew you like me too".* Shane asks, *"do you always taste this sweet? The words coming from your mouth, your voice, just simply your lips... they all taste so sweet."* Mitchie says, *"I really love kissing you...".* He soon stops to catch his breath caressing her cheek softly saying, *"I am sorry, I should have controlled myself".* Mitchie says, *"you don't have to."* Shane says, *"we should go home, fun time is over".* Mitchie nods saying, *"let me tell Nala that we are going home".* Mitchie goes back to the dance floor as Nala says, *"that murder mystery vlogger was so crazy but it's safe now, thanks to me".* Mitchie says, *"thank you Nala, you are truly my bestie".* Nala says, *"I need to catch my flight back to Milan", I will see you again when I finish my shooting".* They hug as Nala whispers in Mitchie's ears, *"don't keep your bodyguard waiting".* Mitchie was stunned saying, *"Nala! Shush!."* Shane watches them wondering, *'what are they whispering about?'.* Soon outside the apartment Mitchie feels exhausted saying, *"I forgot that going to a club is so tiring".* Shane says, *"maybe you are getting older...".* Mitchie smiles saying, *"older and wiser, I'll take that".* Shane turns to open the door saying, *"Mitchie.... did we forget to lock your apartment door?."*

Chapter 14

Mitchie says, *"never!"* Shane opens the door saying, *"stay behind me!"* They head in as Mitchie says, *"MOCO!."* Mitchie heads into the bedroom as Shane comes after her; they find Mocco asleep as Mitchie checks him for injuries or anything; Shane says, *"come with me! let's go check the kitchen."* Mitchie carries Mocco with her as Shane has a search through the kitchen; Mitchie asks, *"did you find anything, Shane?."* Shane replies, *"no, everything looks clean and perfectly normal, we always lock the door."* Mitchie says, *"this is weird."* Mitchie places Mocco down on the chair as her phone beeps looking shocked thinking, *'it's the stalker!.'* She opens the text message, *'Hello Mitchie, I guess you were surprised that you 'forgot' to lock your apartment, rest assured I only snooped around to see the place you are living now and what an adorable dog! I am a little jealous but rest assured that I touched nothing... Good night.'* Mitchie looks at Shane saying, *"it is the stalker! He was in our apartment... Shane, what do we do?! I am so scared; this stalker has gone too far!."* Shane says, *"hey, I am here as long as I am here, nobody can hurt you."* Mitchie wonders, *'I do not feel safe anymore, what if he visits me while I am asleep? I need him with me all the time.'* Mitchie asks, *"can you sleep with me tonight? I am scared if he visits me and hurts me while I am sleeping."* Shane nods replying, *"of course, I will take care of you."* Soon in the bed Mitchie watched as Mocco slept in his bed while looking at Shane saying, *"I can't sleep."* Shane asks, *"are you ok? do you need something?."*

Mitchie answers, *"as long as I have you, it's all good, I am just scared if this stalker comes when I am sleeping."* Shane says, *"I will watch over you, don't worry."* Mitchie says, *"but you need to sleep too, make sure to get some sleep too, ok?."* Shane says, *"your safety is my number one priority not my sleep."* Mitchie says, *"you still need to sleep!."* Shane says, *"I know, just go to sleep."* Mitchie turns and closes her eyes thinking, *'ugh, I cannot sleep.... even though Shane is here, I need him close to me.'* Mitchie opens her asking, *"Shane, can you hug me from behind? I need cuddles."* Shane says, *"really?."* Mitchie says, *"please?."* Shane comes closer and holds her saying, *"like this?."* Mitchie replies, *"yes, I feel safer this way."* Shane says, *"now, go to sleep."* Mitchie says, *"I am trying, Shane."* She turns onto Shane's chest startling him saying, *"cuddle me more!."* Shane says, *"you are such a baby."* Mitchie says, *"I am more comfortable when you are holding me, Good night."* Shane says, *"Good night, Mitchie."* The next morning Mitchie wakes up thinking, *'ugh, it is morning already... I am so tired.'* She gets up and comes downstairs seeing Shane in the kitchen preparing breakfast; she says, *"Good morning, Shane."* Shane answers, *"morning Mitchie, are you ok?"* Mitchie replies, *"just tired, that's all."* Shane serves the toast and fresh juice just as Joanna comes in saying, *"Mitchie, I heard what happened last night from Shane, are you ok? is the apartment not safe anymore? perhaps you should move from this apartment."* Mocco comes in barking as Shane serves him breakfast while Mitchie says, *"maybe you are right, Jo."* Joanna tells Mitchie her schedule for the day as she finishes breakfast and heads upstairs to change. She chooses a white dress and does her hair before coming downstairs with Joanna and Shane however they are soon hounded by a crowd at the entrance as Joanna asks shocked, *"oh no! how did the reporters find us?"* The security guard says, *"please, leave."* A reporter says, *"we will leave after we see Ms Mitchie; we won't be long."* Another says, *"let us see her!"* Mitchie thinks, *'no way!'* Joanna turns to Mitchie saying, *"we have to get out from here."* Shane asks, *"can you run?"* Mitchie replies, *"I am good at running with heels, but I do not want to ruin my dress."* Shane says, *"I will carry you to safety, what do you think?"* Mitchie replies, *"carry me? are you sure?"* Shane nods saying, *"it's faster and safer to avoid those reporters."* Mitchie says, *"alright, you may carry me."* Shane bends down and lifts her saying, *"hold on tight."* They leave via the backdoor as they soon reach the studio where Mitchie says, *"I will put you down now."* Mitchie asks, *"did you have fun?"* Shane replies, *"it's supposed to be my question."* Mitchie says, *"you wanted to carry me, remember?"* Shane says, *"I only did my job, that's all."* Mitchie says playfully, *"always trying to be a professional bodyguard, huh?"* She whispers saying, *"we should do that again."* Shane rolls his eyes saying, *"you are truly an annoying woman."*

Chapter 15

Mitchie looks around before asking, *"where is Joanna?"*. Joanna comes there replying, *"I am going to call our driver, wait here"*. She leaves as Shane looks at Mitchie who asks, *"want to talk about you carried me again?"*. He rolls his eyes saying, *"don't make me regret my decision, please"*. Mitchie giggles saying, *"I can't help it, I love teasing you"*. He sighs saying, *"I should be used to it by now"*. Just then a voice interrupts them saying, *"Mitchie! Are you ok?! What happened? Because I heard from Joanna that reporters were waiting for you"*. Mitchie replies, *"Darren, nothing happened, and everything is under control, what about you?"*. Darren sighs replying, *"yeah, reporters were waiting outside my apartment... I am staying with Richelle, the love of my life. Perhaps you could move apartments or buy a house with fifty bodyguards"*. Mitchie says stunned, *"fifty bodyguard is too much!"*. Darren says, *"for you? No way"*. He looks at Shane asking, *"can I talk to my sister alone, Shane?"*. Shane nods replying, *"I will be right outside"*. Darren says, *"so... is Shane good enough? If he isn't good enough, I can look for another bodyguard for you"*. Mitchie thinks, *'Shane did a good job, and we bonded so well.... I like him, I want him around me'*. Mitchie replies, *"Shane is a very good person, he took care of me very well, he's always watching over me and he is the best"*. Darren says, *"really?"*. Mitchie replies, *"yes, he is! There are a lot of things which happened when we were together, including bad things from the stalker but Shane was always there to protect me, and we bonded as well!"*. Darren asks, *"do you like him, sis?"*. Mitchie was stunned by Darren's question before replying, *"I like him so much, you like him too,*

right?!".Mitchie wonders, *'he didn't mean I like him as in romantically, right?'.* Darren says, *"of course I like him, he has worked with many famous people, and he does his job very well, I am just glad you are safe with him".* Mitchie takes a deep breath before saying, *"I truly like him as a man, not as a bodyguard, are you ok with that, Darren?".*

Darren was stunned by her words saying, *"you do?!".* Mitchie nods while Darren says, *"w-well it's your life... I have no right to say anything about it, I just want my sister to be happy, it's enough for me and I can't bear to know that your life is in danger, I just wish there was someone you could trust to protect you and I am happy if you can trust him or if you like him that much, I won't complain about it, I love you sis and I will always support you.. you are my one and only family, your happiness is my number one priority".* Mitchie hugs Darren unexpectedly saying, *"you are the best brother ever, I love you bro".* Darren says, *"I care about you, ok?".* He hugs her back saying, *"let's stop this awkwardness".* Mitchie says, *"don't be embarrassed! It is normal for us to take of care of each other".* Darren smiles saying, *"thanks for the hug, it's been a while since we hugged, sis".* Mitchie says, *"you always did everything for me, so thank you bro".* They soon head out as Darren says, *"Shane, you take care of my sister very well, ok?".* Shane nods saying, *"of course".* Darren says, *"don't let anyone or anything bother her, ok?".* Shane answers, *"don't worry about it".* Darren says, *"make sure she takes care of herself too".* Shane nervously says, *"y-yes, of course...".* Mitchie rolls her eyes saying, *"Darren, you can be so dramatic!".* Darren says, *"I care about you so much, it's normal, ok?".* Mitchie says, *"I know, but don't worry".* Mitchie turns to Shane saying, *"we are going to do our talk show interviews, bye".* Shane says, *"no need to say goodbye, I am here... always".* On the way to the studio Joanna stops Mitchie saying, *"Mitchie, can we talk before you go into the studio?".* Darren goes ahead with Shane for a moment as Mitchie nods while Joanna says, *"I noticed something between you and Shane, you know it's not good to have something serious with your own bodyguard... it's forbidden, you should think about your status as a celebrity... Shane is nobody, you deserve someone like yourself, someone better and amazing".* Mitchie glares at her thinking, *'how dare she? Really? Shane is nobody? No one should tell me who I should like or date!'.* Mitchie says, *"don't say that about Shane, he is a good person, I cannot believe you said something like this, Joanna... it's my decision who I like, and you can't tell me who I should be seeing, I know Shane is a great person".* Joanna asks, *"you are not thinking about something forbidden, right? We don't need more drama in your life, Mitch".*

Chapter 16

Mitchie folded her arms giving her a cold glare before saying, *"I can control my own life, you do not have to worry about me, I can take care of myself, and I am capable of making decisions for myself".* Joanna says, *"sorry, I was just worried".* She leaves just as Shane comes over to her saying, *"hey, I heard everything".* Mitchie says, *"I-I see....".* Shane says, *"thanks for defending me, honestly you did not have to do that, but I am glad, thanks".* Mitchie says, *"I was just saying the truth".* Shane thanks her as she soon heads over to the studio where the presenter says, *"hello everyone, welcome to the Kylie show! We have the Torres twins right here with us!".* Darren says, *"it's an honour to be back in this show".* Mitchie says, *"thank you for inviting us to your show, Kylie".* Kylie says, *"can we get to the point now? I am curious about your mother's accident; since the fire incident, the media has been all crazy about both of you... especially you, Mitchie! How about a little teatime?".* Mitchie rolled her eyes while looking at Darren who was not comfortable either. Mitchie says, *"rather than talk about gloomy stuff, let's talk about Darren, he is acting in the next Burton's movie, to be able to play in Tim Burton's movie is a dream come true".* Kylie asks, *"right! What will you be playing as, Darren? I heard you will be playing the main character, correct?".* Darren replies, *"I will be playing as Lucifer Morningstar, the devil... he is a devil who in disguise as a mortal trying to look for something interesting".* Mitchie praises Darren saying, *"Darren is so amazing".* Kylie asks, *"how about you, Mitchie? Something you want to share with us?".* Mitchie answers, *"no big plan but I want to work on my new music".* Kylie says, *"sweet! Now, I want to get straight to the point, so Mitchie.. I am curious about your mother's accident; everyone has been so crazy about it all over the news.. what do you think? Since your mother's murderer hasn't been caught yet, he might still be around".*

Darren says, *"you see, Kylie... it was a very traumatic incident for us".* Kylie says, *"tell me what you think, Mitchie"*. Mitchie face becomes angry thinking, *'I can't do this anymore!'.* She gets up saying, *"Stop it! you have no right to talk about my mother's incident! You should stop talking about that right now!".* Kylie says, *"I am sorry, I didn't mean to... I-I was just....c-curious and...".* Darren gets up asking, *"sis, are you ok?".* Mitchie takes a deep breath saying, *"oh no! I ruined the talk show... cut, cut, cut!".* Kylie gets up saying, *"don't worry, this is not a live show".* Mitchie says, *"good to know".* Joanna comes there asking, *"would you like to take a break, Mitchie? We can wait in your dressing room; you don't have to continue this show".* Mitchie thinks, *'it's all my fault that I lost control, but I have to stay professional, I cannot just leave'.* Mitchie turns to Joanna replying, *"that's ok Joanna, I can do this".* Mitchie turns back to Kylie saying, *"I am sorry, can we continue the talk show? I apologise I was carried away with this topic".* Kylie says, *"no I am sorry, I wasn't sensitive about this, I promise I won't mention this topic anymore, can we start over?".* Mitchie nods as Darren says, *"I am so proud of you for being so professional, Mitchie, not everyone can remain professional after being trigged by a sensitive topic. I know this topic triggers you a lot... but I am proud that you can control yourself now, sis".* A few hours later Mitchie felt hungry and wanted the interview to finish quickly; soon in her dressing room Shane asked, *"are you ok? ready to go home?".* Mitchie gets up replying, *"yeah, I guess".* Shane says, *"are you sure, Mitchie? I saw what happened".* Mitchie answers, *"not really".* Shane asks, *"do you want to talk about it? it can be strange to talk about it with me, I mean... it can make you feel uncomfortable. You know, all my life, I lived only with my mother until she passed away, my father left us, and we worked so hard to live through another day, I understand if you feel overprotective over your mother".* Mitchie opens up to Shane saying, *"it's about my mom, you know it already, I just don't want anyone to mention it, it's painful enough to know that she isn't with me and Darren, so I kind of slipped out of control and snapped... ugh I know this is stupid, I must be your most dramatic client, huh?".* Shane asks, *"who said that?".* Mitchie replies, *"I just said that".* Shane says, *"you are not my most dramatic client".* Mitchie says, *"your most cry-baby client?".* Shane shakes his head saying, *"no".* Mitchie says, *"how about weirdest client?".* Shane says, *"hm, I don't know...".* Mitchie says, *"be honest....".*

Chapter 17

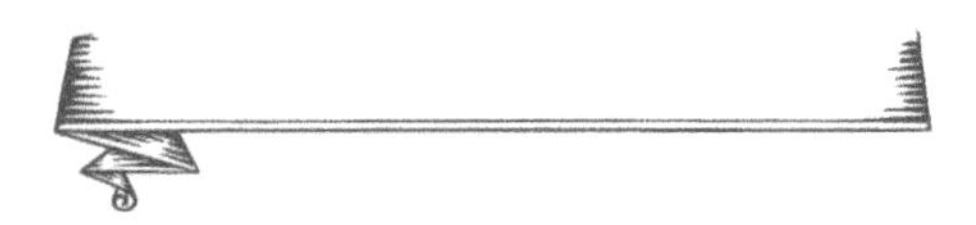

Shane laughs before saying, *"you are fine, ok? you are honest and funny, sometimes you are a little too much though."* Mitchie says, *"that's just my personality, I am glad to have opened to you, it's comforting."* Shane asks, *"so? Want to go home now?."* Mitchie nods saying, *"let's go."* They come out to the lobby where Joanna sees them saying, *"Mitchie, are you going home?."* Mitchie says, *"bye, Joanna."* Joanna says, *"wait, can we talk before you go?."* Mitchie turns back replying, *"sure, I guess."* Shane says, *"I will wait for you outside."* Joanna says, *"you never lose control over yourself on TV shows, I mean... you always control yourself, even if we are talking about your mother, do you want to talk?."* Mitchie coldly replies, *"It's your fault."* Joanna sighs saying, *"if it's about Shane, I am sorry, but I care about you, I want the best for you."* Mitchie says, *"please, I don't want to talk about this right now, I am not angry at you, I just feel a little overwhelmed...."* Joanna was understanding saying, *"but I still don't really think it's a good idea for you to have a little affair with your bodyguard, I am just trying to protect your reputation here."* Mitchie says, *"let's not talk about it, Joanna."* Joanna says, *"ok, I just care about you, get some rest ok?."* Mitchie says, *"of course."*

Mitchie soon comes into the car with Shane saying, *"Joanna has no right to tell me what to do or who I should see! I do not tell her who she should be seeing, and she should not do that to me either!."* Shane says, *"hm...."* Mitchie says, *"and I am hungry now!."* Shane asks, *"do you want to eat somewhere?."* Mitchie replies, *"I don't know, choose a place for me, take me to your favourite place."* Shane thinks, *'my favourite place......'* A few moments later Shane brings her to his favourite Chinese and orders lots of food; Mitchie is excited saying, *"all these dishes look amazing! is this your favourite place?."* Shane nods saying, *"yes, they serve the best food, even though this is just a street snack bar, this is actually my hang out spot with my friends, I know this is not fancy enough for you, but this place brings a lot of memories to me, and I can share this place with you too now".* Mitchie says, *"I am so happy that you showed me this place, perhaps this is going to be my favourite place too."* Shane says, *"ok, whatever you want."* Mitchie uses a chopstick to pick up a dumpling saying, *"let me feed you."* She moves closer as Shane asks stunned, *"why?."* Mitchie says, *"why not?."* Shane says, *"I can eat by myself."* Shane eats it eventually as Mitchie takes a bite of a mooncake saying, *"ok but this mooncake is delicious."* Shane says, *"you are funny, Mitchie."* Mitchie thinks, *'he is so cute when he laughs, it makes me want to kiss him.'* Mitchie comes over and kisses Shane's cheek as he says stunned, *"you enjoy giving me a kiss, I am almost used to it by now."*

Mitchie giggles saying, *"good, get used to it."* They soon come home as Mitchie smiles at Shane saying, *"thanks for always being with me."* Shane says, *"what are you talking about? it's my job."* Mitchie says, *"you know, maybe we should sleep in the same room again, considering someone broke in last time."* Shane says, *"I guess you are right, let's go."* Mitchie teases Shane saying, *"calm down, baby."* Shane rolls his eyes saying, *"you are always teasing me."* Soon Mitchie finishes her shower, changes into her PJs, and sits on her bed thinking, *'I am not excited to sleep... I am not.'* She tries to not smile so much just as Shane comes in asking, *"what are you doing? get into the bed."* Mitchie says, *"I was waiting for you."* Shane says, *"I am here to keep watch, not to sleep with you."* Mitchie says smirking, *"but still, we will be sharing the bed."* Shane says, *"yeah, just get some rest."* They soon lay in the bed as Shane says, *"get some sleep, why are you staring at me like that?".* Mitchie replies, *"because you are so handsome."* Shane says, *"ugh, you are unbelievable, after everything that happened to you today you should get lots of rest, it must have been a stressful day for you, today."* Mitchie nods saying, *"especially the fact that Joanna is suspicious about us, I just wish she didn't have to say anything about you and me, she thinks we have something scandalous."* Shane says, *"well, we should keep everything professional."* Mitchie was annoyed saying, *"I don't like this professionalism thing at all."* Shane says, *"don't think about it and get some rest, the more you think about this the more stressed you will be."* Mitchie says, *"you are right Shane, I should rest, but I don't care about her thoughts anyway."* Shane says, *"hm...."* Mitchie soon feels her eyes heavy and falls asleep; a few hours later she hears Mocco barking as she starts to smell something burning. She opens her eyes shocked wondering, *'what is this smoke?!.'* She turns to the other side of the bed coughing saying, *"I need to find Shane."* Mocco barks again as Mitchie comes out of the bed, opens the door, and sees flame burning all around saying, *"OMG! My apartment is on fire!."*

Chapter 18

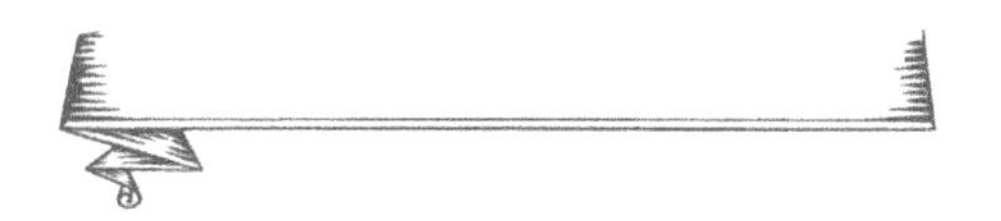

Mitchie coughs due to the heavy smoke and looks around wondering, *'where is Shane?.'* Mitchie screams, *"SHANE!."* Mocco barks as Shane come there saying, *"Mitchie, we have to go now!."* Mitchie says, *"but, my stuff!."* Shane lifts Mocco in his arms saying, *"we have no time! let's go."* They soon run out of the building as a few people gossip outside while Mitchie is with Shane and Mocco in a corner asking, *"how did this happen?."* Shane replies, *"I have no clue, I woke up because of the smoke, and soon it was just fire flames everywhere."* Mitchie looks at Shane asking, *"what should we do?."* Mitchie phones beeps as she sees a text from the unknown, *'Hi Mitchie, did you make it out alive?.'* Mitchie angrily texted, *'you are a pig!.'* The unknown person texts, *'Goodbye, Mitchie, stay alive.'* Mitchie takes a deep breath thinking, *'I knew it.'* Shane understands Mitchie's expression saying, *"It's the psycho, isn't it?."* Mitchie nods replying, *"yep."* Just then Joanna runs there saying, *"Mitchie! Are you alright?! I panicked after you called me, how did this happen?."* Mitchie answers, *"no idea, but I need a place to stay for the night right now."* Shane says, *"you can stay at my place for a while."* Mocco barks as Shane says, *"you too, Mocco!."* Mitchie asks, *"are you sure?."* Shane replies, *"yes, of course."* Joanna says, *"you need a new home though."* Mitchie says, *"we will look tomorrow."* They soon leave and come over to Shane's apartment which is not far; Mitchie looks around inside saying, *"so you live near my apartment, how convenient."* Shane says, *"get some rest, you need it."* Mitchie asks, *"how am I going to*

sleep after the fire incident?." She goes over and sits on the couch looking sad as Shane says, *"are you ok, Mitchie?."*

Mitchie sadly replies, *"no Shane, I lost my apartment and my piano, my piano is my stress reliever."* Shane bends down to her saying, *"hey, I am here to protect you."* Mitchie says, *"I know, but... I can't help but feel anxious."* Shane gets down on his knees saying, *"Mitchie, I am not good at words, but as long as you are with me, you will be fine, I will protect you and I will always save you; do you hear me?."* Mitchie nods saying, *"ok, thanks I needed to hear that."* Shane gets up saying, *"you should get some sleep, you can use my bed, I will take the couch."* Mitchie was hesitant still feeling scared saying, *"Shane, you will sleep with me, ok? I don't think I will be able to sleep properly after that fire incident."* Shane says, *"sure, whatever you want."* Mitchie heads to his room and is stunned thinking with a smile, *'oh, it's a small bed for one person, it's a good thing!.'* Shane comes a few minute after saying, *"sorry, I only have one bed."* Mitchie turned saying happily, *"it is perfect, Shane, let's get into the bed."* Mocco barked as Mitchie says, *"you can sleep at the edge Mocco."* A few moments later they were all in the bed as Mitchie says, *"this bed is truly small."* Shane asks, *"sorry, do you need anything Mitchie?."* Mitchie replies, *"well, you see....."* She comes closer to Shane thinking, *'I don't have to ask him to cuddle me now.'* Shane notices Mitchie close to him saying, *"better?."* Mitchie nods saying, *"better, there is nothing wrong with cuddling and you smell so nice, I love being near you... I feel safe when I am with you, Shane."* Shane says, *"get some sleep, Mitchie, I will be here by your side."* Mitchie yawns saying, *"I am glad you are here with me; I feel so comfortable around you Shane."* She closes her eyes as Shane says, *"me too."* The next morning Mitchie freshened up wearing a causal blouse and jean before heading downstairs. Shane was just finishing preparing food for Mocco as Mitchie came in saying, *"Good morning."* Shane says, *"Good morning, would you like some breakfast?."* Shane prepares a toasted grilled cheese and tomato sandwich and hands it to Mitchie who eats it saying, *"yum!."* After finishing the sandwich and drinking fresh juice Shane asks, *"where do you want to look for an apartment?."* Mitchie answers, *"somewhere near Darren's apartment, not in the same building but near him! He is so protective, and I want my privacy, but at the same time, I want to live near him."* Shane says, *"the apartment needs a very tight security system."* Mitchie says, *"and has to be near my favourite restaurant."* Mocco barks as Mitchie says, *"of course it has to be pet-friendly."* Shane says, *"whatever you want, as long as the security system is good."* Mitchie says, *"let's go! I am super excited to look for a new apartment!."*

Chapter 19

Shane and Mitchie go apartment hunting; after a few places they are finally brought to a building complex; the estate agent says, *"this is our best suite, what do you think?"* Mitchie says, *"let's see...."* She looks around before seeing Shane staring out of the window at the view as Mitchie asks, *"what do you think, Shane?"* Shane replies, *"hmm... it is nice, but it is smaller than your previous apartment, so whatever you like. The security system looks great, though and there's room for a piano which can be good."* Mitchie turns back to the estate agent asking, *"wait before I purchase this apartment, do you allow pets?"* The estate agent nods saying, *"of course, this apartment is pet friendly."* Mitchie smiles saying, *"I will have my manager contact you, I will take this one."* The estate agent says, *"of course, thank you so much, Miss Torres."* Later Mitchie and Shane head over to the studio as Joanna chats with Mitchie saying, *"I am so glad you found a great apartment; I heard Selena Gomez, the famous singer and actress lives there too!"* Mitchie says, *"and the apartment feels so comfortable like a home, maybe because it is not too spacious like before."* Joanna says, *"ok, you need to get ready, the interview is waiting."* Mitchie heads to her dressing room and changes into a simple dress and does her hair and makeup before soon heading out. She takes a seat as Erika says, *"hello Mitchie, let's start this interview."* Mitchie says, *"thanks for having me, Erika, fire the questions away."*

Erika asks, *"can we talk about your love life?"* Mitchie replies, *"sure."* Erika asks, *"so? Are you dating right now?"* Mitchie replies, *"nope."* Erika asks, *"can you tell me your type? A celebrity only? Or you are open to non-celebrity bachelors? do you have a special someone? A secret person you really like?"* Mitchie replies, *"I am open to anyone not a celebrity as long as that person respects me and loves me, it's enough, I don't really think about romance, but I am very open about it."* Erika asks, *"are you the type that waits for her knight in shining armor to come and find you?"* Mitchie answers, *"I prefer to find him myself."* Erika says, *"ooh, nice, so do you have someone special? give me a hint, please?"* Mitchie says, *"I do have someone special in my life."* Erika says, *"OMG! Is he a celebrity? Do we know him? Who is he?"* Mitchie answers, *"you don't know him, nobody knows him, and he is not a celebrity."* Erika says, *"a normal person?"* Mitchie nods while Erika says, *"so a normal person out of the spotlight can have Mitchie's heart, what a humble and kind-hearted person you are, Mitchie, I believe many people will fall in love with you more after this statement, ooh this is good to hear."* Soon outside Joanna is with Shane talking saying, *"I am so sorry, Shane."* Shane's facial expression looks sad as Mitchie comes over saying, *"hey, what's going on?"*

Joanna replies, *"I am going to replace Shane with a new bodyguard for you."* Mitchie was shocked and thought, *'WHAT?'* Mitchie says, *"NO!"* Joanna says, *"the new bodyguard is better and has more experience, you will be safer, they have been a lot of accidents happening, and I think we need someone who has more experience."* Mitchie says, *"but Shane is experienced!"* Shane says, *"perhaps I should wait outside and let both of you talk."* Mitchie says, *"No! you stay!"* Joanna says, *"I think it's better if Shane waits outside, I want to talk about both of you."* Mitchie says annoyed, *"just say it!"* Joanna says, *"ok, I can see that Shane is making a move on you, you are a celebrity after all."* Mitchie says, *"it was me! Not him!"* Joanna says, *"it is better if both of you stop seeing each other, it is to avoid scandals! You know how the press can get; you have already faced enough problems."* Shane says, *"Joanna is right."* Mitchie became defensive saying, *"no! Shane is not a problem, you know nothing about him Joanna and please do not agree with her, Shay... I would rather be with Shane, and I am comfortable with him, you should know that I do not really get comfortable with many people, Joanna! Now you want to replace Shane... also might I remind you Darren is the one who hired him, not you, so it is not your choice to fire him like this."* Joanna says, *"I am your manager and I want the best for you, Mitchie... this is a genuine issue, ok? Do not risk your reputation and image for this."* Mitchie says, *"I do not agree on this, Shane is an amazing guy, ok?! You should know that I do not like bodyguard, but Shane is different."* Joanna says, *"if I told you before, you would have disagreed with me!"* Mitchie says, *"I disagree with you now!"* Joanna pleads saying, *"the new bodyguard will be here tomorrow, consider today as your last day with Shane."* Joanna walks away as Shane comes over saying, *"thank you for defending me."*

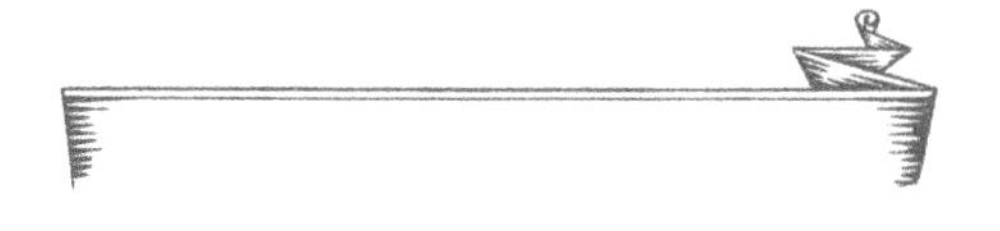

Chapter 20

Mitchie says, *"this is not fair!"* Shane says, *"hey, it will be fine, we still have today, and I am happy you disagree with Joanna, it means something to me."* Mitchie says, *"I only said the truth."* Shane says, *"we can do something else today, if you want to."* Mitchie says, *"that's a great idea, let's get out of here."* Shane brings Mitchie to the aquarium as Shane says, *"I really like it around here, seeing the fish swimming peacefully, hearing the sound of water and seeing how they create bubbles with their fins and pops, it's relaxing."* Mitchie says, "aww, you sound so poetic." Mitchie runs around to every glass window and calls Shane who says, *"you are acting like a little baby."* Mitchie turns to face him smiling saying, *"maybe I am your little baby."* A few moments later Shane tells her to slow down as Mitchie says, *"I am excited, ok?"* Soon in a quiet corner he holds Mitchie against the glass window as she asks, *"what are you doing?"* Shane caresses her cheek softly replying, *"you look so cute, you make me want to kiss you."* Mitchie says, *"kiss me, now."* They kiss gently as things begin to get passionate as Mitchie says, *"someone will see us."* Shane asks, *"you don't mind, right?"* Mitchie replies, *"I don't care at all."* Shane says, *"good or do you prefer somewhere more private?"* Mitchie replies, *"anywhere you want."* They stop to catch their breath as Shane says, *"I guess we have to go now."*

Mitchie says, *"I guess so too."* They head back to the new apartment as he immediately kisses her passionately as she holds him closer; he says, *"I can't get enough of you."* Mitchie says, *"take me to your bed now!"* Shane asks, *"are you sure?"* Mitchie replies, *"yes!"* They remove their clothes as Shane lays her on the bed and kisses her passionately saying, *"I want you, every inch of you...."* Mitchie asks, *"what are you waiting for?"* They get intimate in every touch and every moment as Mitchie says, *"Shane...."* Shane answers, *"yes?"* Mitchie says, *"I like you a lot...."* Shane says, *"you taste so sweet."* Mitchie moans Shane's name as he says, *"I like it when you say my name with your soft voice."* Mitchie says, *"I want more of you...."* Shane says, *"I like you too, Mitchie... a lot, you are the most gorgeous girl I have ever seen."* Mitchie says, *"and you make me feel that way tonight."* They stop as Shane caresses her face saying, *"I can do this all night."* Mitchie asks, *"then why did you stop?"* Shane answers, *"because, I don't want to keep you awake all night."* Mitchie teases him as he tickles her and then kisses her again as they make love all through the night.

The next day Mitchie wakes up feeling tired and heads to the bathroom to freshen up choosing to wear something casual." She comes out to see Shane in the living room in his boxers as Mitchie says, *"I really do not want to lose you, Shane... I need you; I cannot lose you."* Shane says, *"you will be fine, Mitchie, this is not the end of the world."* Mitchie says, *"you don't understand...."* Mocco barks as Joanna knocks on the door; Shane opens it as Joanna comes in saying, *"let me introduce you to your new bodyguard."* A guy comes behind her saying, *"Hi, I am Alexander."* Mitchie thinks sadly, *'this is it; I will not see Shane anymore.... I cannot do this; I do not want to lose him.'* Joanna asks, *"Mitchie, are you ok?"* Mitchie replies irritated, *"no, I am not ok!"* Joanna apologizes as Mitchie says, *"I need time."* She heads out while Shane says, *"I will talk to her."* Joanna says, *"ok, thank you for all your work, Shane, you are a good person... I wish you luck in your future career."* Shane thanks her, goes to his room and changes before heading to the park. He finds Mitchie on the bridge saying, *"here you are."* Mitchie turns asking, *"why are you here, Shane?"* Shane answers, *"looking for you, of course."* Mitchie says, *"I am sorry I made such a big deal about this."* Shane says, *"no that's totally ok, you should head back."* Mitchie sighs sadly saying, *"and lose you?"* Shane says, *"hey, I am not going anywhere, it's just that I won't be working with you that's all, it's not the end of the world... we will meet again."* Mitchie says, *"yeah."* They look into each other's eyes as Mitchie comes closer to Shane kissing him thinking, *'this may be our last kiss....'* She says, *"I don't want to lose you."* Shane says, *"you will be fine."* They stop as Shane says, *"go back to Joanna, ok?"* Mitchie says, *"I will miss you."* Shane says, *"I will miss you, too."* Mitchie says, *"you have my number, call me anytime?"* Shane says, *"perhaps, I will, good luck with your life Mitchie."* Mitchie says, *"you too, Shane."* They soon part way in opposite directions.

Chapter 21

Mitchie comes home thinking, *'and here's to a new day without Shane'.* Joanna asks, *"Mitchie, are you ok?".* Mitchie replies, *"no".* Joanna says, *"today, we have a photoshoot for Glamour Magz, I am going to get my stuff and we are going, ok?".* Joanna leaves as Alexander says, *"do not do something stupid, always stay in my sight, don't run away... behave yourself and be professional".* Mitchie says, *"shall we be friends? A good relationship starts with a good friendship, how long have you been a bodyguard?".* Alexander coldly replies, *"I don't have to answer that question to you, you don't have to talk to me and vice versa".* Mitchie thinks, *'seriously? What's with the rude tone?'.* Mitchie says, *"you don't have to be rude".* Mocco barks and growls at him as he says, *"I am not here to be nice, is that why you liked your last bodyguard so much? Because he was nice? I guess that's why he couldn't protect you better since both of you were playing around".* Mitchie thinks, *'OMG! Damn, he is so rude! I couldn't stand this attitude! I need to stand my ground!'.* Mitchie firmly says, *"don't you dare speak to me like that! you are working under me, you are just my bodyguard. You have no right to speak to me like that or to anyone else! If I were you, I would watch my tone".* Alexander says, *"or what?".* Mitchie says, *"I will fire you! and I don't care about what Joanna or anyone else thinks, you won't say anything bad about me, or my last bodyguard, understand? And you'd better watch your tone every time you speak to me, because I am still your Boss... got it?".*

Alexander replies, *"got it, I am sorry".* Mitchie says, *"thank you, apology accepted".* Joanna comes back saying, *"I am ready, let's go".*

Mitchie says, *"I am sorry Joanna, I don't feel like doing it"*. Joanna says stunned, *"what?! but!"*. Mitchie says, *"yes, cancel everything, I want to spend my day with my brother today, that's final"*. Joanna says, *"fine"*. Joanna leaves as Mitchie says to Alexander, *"and I can take care of myself"*. He says, *"I am your bodyguard, I will follow you"*. Mitchie rolls her eyes saying, *"whatever"*. She leaves and soon drives over to the studio where her brother is in the middle of filming; Mitchie sits and waits for Darren who soon comes over as Mitchie says, *"cool acting, bro"*. Darren asks, *"are you proud of me, sis?"*. Mitchie replies, *"you are amazing, Darren"*. Darren says, *"thanks, are you ok? I mean you rarely visit me on my film set"*. Mitchie says, *"I just wanted to see you, that's all... you always seem so happy-go-lucky"*. Darren replies, *"why not? it's in my nature"*. Just then a woman comes over saying, *"Darren, Chloe is looking for you... don't keep your lover waiting!"*. Darren leaves as the woman comes over to her saying, *"hello Mitchie, how can I help you today?"*. Mitchie thinks, *'Sarah is Darren and Chloe's manager'*. Mitchie says, *"hey Sarah, I have a question for you, does Darren get hate mail from his fans?"*. Sarah answers, *"no, I read all of his fan mail and I handle all of his social media, I burn every fan mail, either good or bad and I delete all negative comments in his social media, I hate humans and I will curse anyone that touch Darren or Chloe's peace, as long as I am there no one can touch them"*. Mitchie was taken back surprised saying, *"um.... woah that sounds... a little scary"*. Mitchie wonders, *'so this is why Darren is always so calm and happy'*. Mitchie compliments Sarah saying, *"you are amazing for doing all of these works, Sarah"*. Just then Sarah's phone rings and she goes to attend the call as Mitchie goes to look for Darren and tells him everything. Darren says, *"Shane has been replaced? If Joanna thinks that's the best, then I agree with her"*. Mitchie shares her doubts with Darren as he reassures her, *"he is just a bodyguard, he can't do anything stupid"*. Mitchie says, *"you're right, bro"*. Just then someone comes over saying, *"Jess couldn't make it to the set! We need someone to replace her!"*. Darren says, *"I know the perfect replacement for Jess!"*.

Mitchie sees her brother looking at her asking, *"why are you looking at me?!"*. The director comes over saying, *"superb, superb you can be Jess, I mean the evil Olivia role... chop, chop and go get ready female Torres"*. Darren says, *"it will be so fun, Mitch, let's do this!"*. Mitchie ponders for a moment before saying, *"let's do this!"*.

Chapter 22

Mitchie does the scene with Darren as the director soon screams, *"CUT!"* He comes over saying, *"superb. Female Torres I did not know that you can act too, which is a good thing... I should consider you to be the main character for my next movie, thanks you."* He leaves screaming, *"next scene! Let us go!"* Mitchie smiles as Darren says, *"look at you! Not all people can impress him, you know how meticulous he is with actors and actresses, you are going to steal my job now."* Mitchie says, *"it's in Torres's blood to be an actress or actor."* Soon in the dressing room Mitchie meets Chloe who says, *"hey, Mitchie I am glad you visited Darren and me today, I wish we could talk more, but I need to shoot for my scene."* Mitchie says, *"that's ok, I am here just to say that you are amazing, and I am glad you are with my brother."* Chloe hugs her saying, *"you can change into one of my outfits before you head home."* Soon Mitchie comes out as Alexander asks, *"so? Ready to go home?"* Mitchie replies, *"let's stop somewhere, I need to get myself a meal."*

Alexander rolls his eyes saying, *"whatever."* They drive to a restaurant as Mitchie heads in saying, *"hi, can I have spaghetti bolognaise for takeout, please?"* The server replies, *"sure."* She leaves as a familiar person appears behind Mitchie calling out her name. Mitchie turns surprised saying, *"Shane! I did not expect to see you here and again."* Shane says, *"me too, what a small world we live in."* Mitchie says, *"you look good, how are you?"* Shane replies, *"great, you?"* Mitchie smiles saying, *"good, I feel so happy to see you again... I miss you."* Shane says, *"I miss you too."* Mitchie asks, *"what do you do? Still in a bodyguard job?"* Shane replies, *"actually I am on a break right now, I was just seeing my friends and now, taking a dinner out."* Mitchie looks around as Shane asks, *"what are you doing?"* Mitchie replies, *"can we find a quieter place to talk?"* Shane asks confused, *"why?"* Mitchie says, *"I will explain."* Shane says, *"let's go."* Soon in a quiet spot Shane asks, *"so, what's going on?"* Mitchie replies, *"I don't want my bodyguard to see us together."* Shane says, *"ah, I understand, why? Did he do something to you?"* Mitchie says, *"it's about Alexander, my new bodyguard, I feel uncomfortable around him, and he was rude to me, he even badmouthed you and me, I don't want to see him, Joanna picked the wrong bodyguard."* Shane says, *"if I understand correctly....so, you miss working with me, huh?"* Mitchie replies smiling, *"very much, don't you miss working with me too?"* Shane replies, *"what kind of answer do you want?"*

Mitchie says, *"something that makes me happy, very happy."* Shane says, *"then yes, I miss working with you too."* Mitchie says, *"really? Prove it."* He comes closer and caresses her cheek saying, *"like what?"* Mitchie teases him saying, *"a kiss?"* Shane kisses her forehead as she blushes saying, *"I'll take that forehead kiss."* Shane says, *"as you should."* Just then Alexander comes saying, *"Miss Torres, let's go, I have your dinner with me."* Mitchie sighs saying, *"ok, I must go... I will see you around."* They soon come out the restaurant to find a crowd of reporter waiting for them; Mitchie was stunned saying, *"no!"* Alexander comes in front saying, *"sorry, but please don't disturb Mitchie."* Mitchie panics thinking, *'oh no, I should go somewhere safe.'* Just then someone's arm wraps around her waist and takes her away as she is standing against the wall saying, *"Shane!"* Shane says, *"hey."* He is still holding her as she asks, *"w-what are you doing?"* Shane replies, *"I saved you, didn't I?"* Mitchie smirks playfully saying, *"I guess."* Shane says, *"you were in trouble, so I just stepped in to save you, you are welcome."* Mitchie teases him saying, *"or maybe an excuse to be alone with me?"* Shane says, *"maybe."* Mitchie tells him, *"So tell me what your intention is... Mr. Gray."* Shane says, *"let's see... Miss Torres, there is only one thing I want."* He holds and pulls her gently towards him whispering, *"you."* Mitchie notices Shane being sweet as she says smiling, *"if you want to kiss me, do it now, before I change my mind."* Shane kisses her as Mitchie says, *"mmm, I can see you like to kiss me now."* Shane says, *"you taste like candy, I could kiss you all day."* Mitchie is mesmerized by his words saying, *"look at you, you sound so adorable right now."* Shane winks at her playfully as she says, *"I wish you were still around me."* Shane asks, *"what are you talking about, Mitchie? I will always be here."* Mitchie says, *"yes, it is just... I will not see you every day, so it is killing me a little."* Shane says, *"you'll survive."* Mitchie says, *"now, I can't wait to see you again."* Alexander comes there saying, *"the reporters have left, we can go now."* Mitchie says, *"that's my cue to leave."* Shane says, *"see you around, Mitchie."* Mitchie and Alexander head to the car as he says, *"really?"* Mitchie says, *"what?"* Alexander had a cold tone saying, *"you are always clinging on to him, he is not your bodyguard anymore."* Mitchie says, *"you are not my dad!"* Alexander says, *"you shouldn't get involved with him."* Mitchie asks, *"why?"* Alexander angrily replies, *"because I am your bodyguard, and you will listen to me!."*

Chapter 23

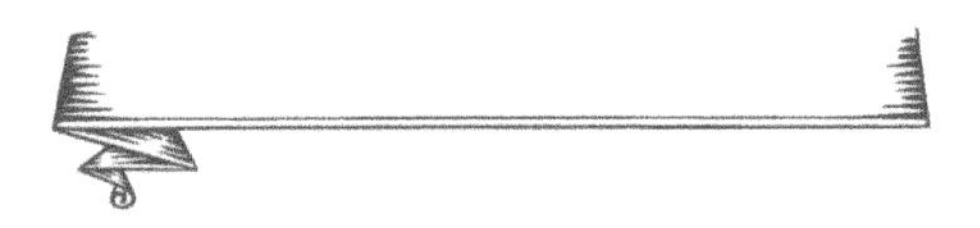

Mitchie says irritated, *"you know what, I am done arguing with you, I am going home with Shane!".* Alexander was stunned saying, *"No! you can't! you cannot be serious, I'm doing my job".* Mitchie says, *"I am not going to listen to you".* Mitchie runs off and soon sees Shane going into his car as she calls out, *"SHANE!."* Shane turns to see Mitchie who asks, *"can you give me a ride home?."* Shane replies, *"are you ok, Mitchie?".* Mitchie sighs answering, *"I don't want to be in the same car as Alexander".* Shane nods saying, *"alright, you can come with me".* They both get in as Shane drives while Mitchie says, *"ugh, he is so annoying! I can't stand him anymore!"* Shane says, *"Joanna would be angry if you didn't go with him".*

Mitchie says, *"I would rather have Joanna angry with me than to be in the same car as Alexander, atleast I get to spend more time with you, so it's all good".* Shane places his hand on Mitchie and gives her a smile before soon driving off. Mitchie comes to her apartment opening the door saying, *"Mocco I'm home".* She comes into the living room to see a familiar person waiting for her as she says surprised, *"Joanna!."* Joanna gets up from the couch saying, *"hey, I am just checking your apartment".* Mitchie says, *"and? Tell me everything."* Joanna says, *"I saw you with Shane in the restaurant, what were you doing with him?"* Mitchie says, *"you are just seeing things, there's no way you saw me".* Joanna says, *"I know what I saw, did you two do something? You know, it's better to not try to stay away from Alexander... he is your bodyguard, and he only wants to protect you".* Mitchie says annoyed, *"he is a jerk, do you know that?"*. Joanna says, *"remember tolerance and patience"*. Mitchie says, *"ok...."* Joanna says, *"also yesterday, you can't just cancel your schedule! Do you know who you cancelled? Justin Timberland, the famous pop singer!"* Mitchie says, *"what did he want from me?!"*. Joanna replies, *"I think he wants to collaborate with you"*. Mitchie was surprised and excited at the same time as Joanna says, *"it was your fault, you cancelled the meeting yesterday"*.

Mitchie sighs saying, *"sorry, I just needed to clear my head yesterday, but I am ready to meet him"*. Mitchie hears the doorbell ring as she says, *"I will get the door"*. She goes and opens it looking at the corridor saying, *"huh? Hello?"* There is no one around as Joanna comes asking, *"is everything alright, Mitchie?"*. Mitchie replies, *"no, this is spooky and strange."* Joanna says, *"I should head home now but I can stay if you want me to."* Mitchie says, *"no it's ok, I have Mocco, and we will both be fine"*. Joanna nods saying, *"see you tomorrow then"*. Joanna leaves as Mitchie locks her door and checks everywhere before grabbing Mocco and heading to bed; The next day Mitchie gets up as she gets changed, feeds Mocco and then heads out. Justin says, *"I am so glad you came, follow me to the studio"*. Mitchie tells Alexander to stay in the room as she follows Justin to his studio as he says, *"sorry, my studio is not as big as expected!"*. Mitchie disagreed saying, *"no, it's perfect"*. Justin goes to get the lyrics for his song and hands it to her as she reads it and tries to find the melody. Justin asks, *"so what do you think? Also, would you like to add anything?"*. Mitchie gives her suggestion as Justin says, *"that sounds amazing, let me fix the lyrics and show you the music arrangements, I am so happy to collab with you, this will be brilliant, when I wrote the lyrics, I knew Mitchie Torres was the best person to collab with"*. Mitchie says, *"thank you for trusting me"*. Mitchie smiles at Justin as she soon says, *"I need to use the restroom"*. Justin says, *"it's at the end of the hallway"*. Mitchie says, *"I will be right back"*. As she heads down the corridor, she looks around seeing various paintings wondering, *'wow he sure is rich'*. A voice suddenly interrupts her thoughts as she turns to see Shane who says, *"Mitchie? What are you doing here?"* Mitchie turned surprised saying, *"OMG! You are here."* Shane says, *"Justin hired me last night, only for a short time and the payment is pretty nice".* Mitchie says, *"aww I missed you; I am so happy to see you".* Shane comes closer and carries her saying, *"come with me."* He brings her to a closet as he kisses her warmly as she says, *"mmm, I can see that you miss me too".* Shane says, *"you sound a little cocky".* They stop as Mitchie says, *"only stating the truth".* Shane caresses her cheek saying, *"but, you are right".* Shane says, *"I miss you."* Mitchie says, *"Justin can wait, kiss me."* They both kiss each other passionately as Shane gets worried while Mitchie says, *"five minutes...".* Soon Shane lets Mitchie head back to the studio as Justin says, *"let's try our first recording session".*

Chapter 24

The rest of the day was spent with Mitchie recording the new song with Justin. Justin says, *"you were awesome, Mitchie! Sorry, I have to go right now... we can continue another day and I will record my part and show you"*. Mitchie says, *"thank you for this amazing experience!"*. Justin walks out with Mitchie as it is dark in the street; he asks, *"where is your bodyguard?."* Mitchie replies, *"he is on his way, don't worry."* Shane comes saying, *"let's go, Justin."* He nods as an unknown person in a hoodie comes pointing the gun saying, *"you are going to die!."* Shane says, *"look out!."* Mitchie freezes as the unknown person fires a shot which hits Justin who screams, *"AH!"*. Justin drops to the ground as Shane runs, punches the unknown person, and takes the gun pointing it at him saying, *"get down!"*. Justin gets up as Mitchie asks, *"are you ok?"*. Justin replies, *"h-he shot my arm!."* Mitchie takes out her mobile phone saying, *"I am going to call an ambulance and police!."* Justin thanks Mitchie as a few moments later the paramedics take Justin while the police officers take the shooter away. Mitchie asks, *"are you ok?."* Justin replies, *"don't worry about me, worry about Shane."* Alexander comes saying, *"what's going on? I heard gunshots!."* Mitchie thinks, *'is this it? is the stalker finally caught? I hope this is the end.'* Soon at the hospital Justin decides to cancel the show and recover while Shane insist to stay by his side however Justin says, *"no need, you should take care of Mitchie, she seems a little shaken up right now"*. Mitchie says, *"I am totally fine!."* Justin says, *"I will probably lose my ability to write songs!."*

Mitchie says, *"DON'T SAY THAT!."* Shane apologises saying, *"I am sorry, I couldn't protect you, I-I failed you".* Justin says, *"I understand the situation, you should focus on protecting a woman first".* Later outside the hospital Shane asks, *"Mitchie, are you alright?".* Mitchie replies, *"I am fine, Shane... I should wait for Alexander; he's dealing with the shooter."* Shane asks, *"are you sure? I will drive you home if you like or you can stay at my place, you are still in shock."* Mitchie nervously says, *"well... I want to stay with you at your place, I don't want to be alone tonight".* Shane takes her hand saying, *"that's ok, I am here.. let's go."* They soon reach the apartment as Mitchie says, *"the place is still the same".* Shane asks, *"would you like anything?."* Mitchie yawns replying, *"a good night sleep, thanks Shane... I am tired."* Shane comes closer holding her waist saying, *"I am glad that you are ok, I cannot imagine something bad happening to you, I will lose my mind".* Mitchie says playfully, *"then, what are you going to do now?".* Shane says, *"you tell me."* Mitchie replies, *"spend the night with me."* Shane kisses Mitchie and lifts her in his arms as she wraps her legs around him and he carries her to the bedroom. They remove their clothes and kiss under the duvet as Shane says, *"I could never get enough of you, what have you done to me Mitchie?".* Mitchie replies, *"I am insatiable! I always want you, you always calm me down, protect me and I like you a lot."* Shane says, *"I like you too, Mitchie".*

The next day Mitchie borrows Shane's clothes and comes to the kitchen seeing Shane cook her breakfast as she says, *"thanks for the clothes, I have to leave before Joanna or Alexander worry about me".* Shane says, *"wait, are you heading the hospital?".* Mitchie replies, *"yep, I will visit Justin."* Shane says, *"I will see you at the hospital then, be careful".* Mitchie nods and kisses him before soon heading to the hospital and checking on Justin who was recovering well. Shane says, *"are you going to be ok?".* Justin replies, *"yes, I can go home tomorrow, it's not a big deal".* Justin notices something between Shane and Mitchie however soon changes the topic asking, *"have you had any information on the shooter?."* Shane replies, *"perhaps we will hear something today?".*

Justin says, *"I still want to work with you, Mitchie Torres".* Mitchie was stunned saying, *"are you sure? I thought that this issue will put you off."* Justin was understanding and says, *"you are a talented individual, and it would be my loss to lose you".* Mitchie thanks him as an officer soon comes in with information on yesterday's shooting however they all shocked by what the officer tells them about the shooter. Mitchie is worried saying, *"he's not the stalker, but a runaway criminal?".* Mitchie's phone beeps as she sees an incoming text from the stalker who says, *'it's not the end yet'.*

Chapter 25

Mitchie thinks, *'no way! This cannot be true! He is still around... it's not over....'* The officer notices Mitchie asking, *"is something wrong, Miss Torres?".* Mitchie replies, *"do you have an update about the fire incident at my concert and apartment? I need to know what truly happened."* The officer replies, *"to be honest, we are still investigating this issue, but one thing for certain is this is no accident, even CCTV was not working that day, this appears to be all planned".* Mitchie asks, *"what should I do now? I don't feel safe at all now."* The officer replies, *"we are trying our best to crack this case, for now please be careful and always have someone around you to protect you".* Mitchie nods saying, *"thank you so much for letting me know".* He leaves as Shane says, *"hey, we are in this together, I will protect you".* Mitchie says, *"I still can't sleep peacefully at night".* Shane reassures her that they will get through this together as Mitchie appreciates Shane's presence and comforting words. Justin says, *"so, he is just a runaway criminal and not the one who has been terrorising, Mitchie."* Shane says, *"I am going to stay here with Justin, do you have any work schedule today, Mitchie?".* Mitchie replies, *"I need to ask Joanna about that".* Shane asks, *"do you want me to drive you back to your apartment?".* Mitchie replies, *"that's ok, I will call Joanna to pick me up, stay here with Justin".* Justin claims he is fine however Mitchie insists that Shane stay by his side. Shane says, *"call me if something happens."* Mitchie nods and leaves as Justin says, *"isn't she special?".* Shane smiles replying, *"yeah...."* Mitchie comes to her apartment and is stunned to find Alexander waiting for her as she says, *"oh!".*

Alexander asks, *"Miss Torres, where have you been?!".* Mitchie replies, *"I am here."* Alexander says, *"this is not the right time to joke around."* Mitchie says, *"I just visited Justin because he was injured, what about you? I haven't seen you until today."* Alexander answers, *"I was with the police the whole night, I visited your apartment this morning and I saw you left your place, I decided to wait until your return".* Mitchie says, *"sneaky, huh?."* Alexander rolls his eyes saying, *"Joanna is waiting for you in the kitchen".* Mitchie comes to the kitchen to find Mocco eating while Joanna sees Mitchie who looks surprised. Mitchie says, *"Joanna?."* Joanna says, *"Mitchie! Are you ok?!."* Mitchie replies calmly, *"don't panic, I am fine."* Joanna says, *"gosh! I was so worried about you! I heard what happened, it's all over the news! I am so glad you are fine."* Mitchie says, *"thanks to Shane!."* Joanna says, *"I get it, I want to apologise for making you and Shane stay apart, perhaps you are right that Shane is the best person for you... he always protects you and always there to help, I will try to ask Shane to work with us again... will you forgive me, Mitchie? I feel like I owe you an apology, I understand if you don't want to accept my apology... I won't force you."* Mitchie sighs as Joanna says, *"I decided to stay with you and Mocco tonight, you need someone to look after you and I am here for you both".* Mocco barks happily while Joanna says, *"you're right, I need you here... I don't want to be alone tonight."* The next day Mitchie gets up and sees Joanna in the kitchen with Mocco saying, *"good morning Joanna, I am going to visit Shane at his apartment today".* Joanna says, *"ok, see you."* Soon Mitchie and Shane are discussing about a plan to find the stalker as Shane says, *"I have a suggestion".* Mitchie asks, *"hmm, what is it?."* Shane asks, *"do you want to learn how to defend yourself a little?".* Mitchie thought for a moment and nodded before soon practising with Shane a few simple punches and kicks. Shane was impressed as he tried overpower her however Mitchie tripped him and then pinned him down to the floor as their eyes met. They soon shared a passionate kiss as Shane lifts her and brings her to his bed where they make love; later that evening on the terrace Shane looked out at the sky as Mitchie came over saying, *"did Joanna call you? we had a talk last night and we want you back".* Shane replies, *"yeah, she called me, but I rejected the offer."* Mitchie was stunned saying, *"but why?!."* Shane answers, *"I don't want to be your bodyguard anymore, right now I want to be someone who is equal with you, not someone who works with you, but only me... by working with you, I feel like there's a boundary I must not cross, I prefer things just as they are right now".* Mitchie smiles saying, *"aw, Shane.. I want to be with you all the time."* Shane caresses her cheek saying, *"I will always be here for you, and I will always protect you, when everything is over we can be together freely".* Mitchie says, *"you cutiepie!."* Shane kisses her saying, *"you should go home, it's getting late."* Mitchie nods while Shane says, *"I will come over to dinner at your place soon".*

Chapter 26

Mitchie comes home to find Alexander waiting for her as she says, *"you can go home, Alexander, I will be fine alone"*. Alexander says, *"Joanna called me, and she said she wanted to replace me, huh? are you going to take Shane back?"*. Mitchie replies, *"why are you angry about it?"*. Alexander says, *"because it's not fair!."* Mitchie says, *"w-why?."* Alexander says angrily, *"because you can't get rid of me! I have to be by your side, you won't understand!."* Mitchie asks confused, *"w-what do you mean?."* Alexander replies, *"I won't hand you to another person while you are already in front of me!"*. He sends a text message from his phone as Mitchie's phone beeps and sees the text from the stalker. Mitchie says, *"Alexander?."* Alexander replies, *"yes, Mitchie! You are mine!."* Mitchie is shocked thinking, *'no! Alexander is my stalker! He is right in front of me...'* Mitchie says, *"you have to calm down!."* Alexander says, *"not this time!."* Mocco comes in as he barks angrily seeing Alexander whilst Mitchie uses the opportunity to run away; Alexander yells, *"YOU CAN'T RUN AWAY FROM ME!"*. Mocco bites his leg as Alexander kicks him against the wall saying, *"disgusting fleabag!"*. Mitchie runs down a few metres in the corridor before not being able to run any further. Alexander appears behind her as Mitchie punches him however he shoves her to the floor saying, *"you are not going anywhere! We will end everything here!."* Mitchie asks, *"why are you doing this?!."* Alexander warns her, *"shut up! you can't run away from me anymore"*. He drugs her before carrying her away; a few hours later she wakes up to find herself tied to the char as she says, *"why are you doing*

this to me?!". Alexander replies, *"This is my revenge to your bitchy mother! I loved her, I was truly in love with her until she got pregnant! And she had kids! I had to kill her; I had no choice to kill her! she was no longer my pure Kaitlyn!"*. Mitchie asks, *"can I know what happened? please tell me everything about my mother"*.

Alexander replies, *"I will consider this your final request"*. Alexander narrates how he was mesmerized by Kaitlyn's charisma and beauty and how he as a fan adored her however he soon find out about her pregnancy in which he turned cold and ruthless claiming Kaitlyn was no longer *'pure and innocent'*. Alexander remembers coming to her apartment thinking, *'if I can't have her, then nobody can'*. Mitchie coldly says, *"you are a sick disgusting person!"*. Alexander says, *"how dare she betray me?!"*. Mitchie replies, *"you were just her fan, you had no right to take her life!"*. Alexander says, *"no one can touch her but me!"*. Mitchie thinks, *'he's crazy, mental, and an obsessive fan! My mom had to be his victim.'* Mitchie asks, *"one last question? Who is my father? Are you my father?"*. Alexander replies, *"why do you want to know? you are going to die anyway... your mother is a slut!"*. Mitchie gets defensive saying, *"don't you dare speak about her that way!."* Alexander says, *"the fact that you are here and alive right now is proof that she is a bitch! And you... you look so much like my dear Kaitlyn... I have to kill you! and your brother too! I will kill and destroy all of the people that are connected to my Kaitlyn"*. Mitchie says, *"YOU ARE A PYSCHO!."* Alexander slaps her saying, *"SHUT UP! I WILL KILL YOU RIGHT NOW!."* Mitchie had tears in her eyes as he cocked the gun and aimed it at her; he says, *"Goodbye, Mitchie Torres"*. Mitchie closed her eyes as a bullet was fired however she opened her eyes and saw someone else holding the gun and pointing it at Alexander. Alexander was on the floor as Shane dropped the gun and looked at Mitchie asking, *"hey, are you ok?"*. Mitchie replies, *"I am ok."* Shane unties the rope saying, *"thank god, you are ok Mitchie"*. Mitchie gets up saying, *"Alexander!."* They look around to see that he has escaped; Shane says, *"let's focus on you!"*. Soon in her apartment the officers were around while Mocco slept on the couch. Despite officers trying to take Mitchie somewhere else to be safe she insisted on staying at her apartment with Shane. The officer decided to leave a few of his men to guard the doors and be on alert. A few days later Mitchie is still wondering about Alexander and his next moves as Shane comes in saying, *"Mitchie, Joanna is here"*. Joanna runs and hugs Mitchie saying, *"OMG! Are you alright?!."* Mitchie says, *"I am fine"*. Joanna asks, *"Shane, can you take care of Mitchie?"*. Mocco barks as Joanna says, *"I am sorry I have been busy these past few days, my mother is in town, and I cannot leave her alone at my apartment"*. Shane replies, *"yes, you can count on me"*. Mitchie's phone beeps as she sees a text from Alexander who says, *'this is not the end, Mitchie! I will be back for you.'*

Chapter 27

Mitchie says, *"I don't need to his messages."* Shane says, *"you should turn off your phone, it's not good for you to see those things".* Mitchie says, *"yeah and now I just want to rest".* Shane says, *"as long as I am here, nothing will happen to you, ok?".* Mitchie smiles and thanks him as he says, *"we are in this together".* Mocco barks as Mitchie giggles saying, *"with you Shane, I have no doubt".* The next day Mitchie wakes up restless for not having much sleep as Shane comes over saying, *"Good morning, how did you sleep?".* Mitchie replies, *"terribly!."* He asks, *"do you need more rest? How can I rest when Alexander is still out there?".* Mitchie has some breakfast with Mocco as she thinks of something and says, *"Shane, I've just had an idea".* Shane replies, *"idea? What is it?."* Mitchie says, *"I am going to send a challenge video to Alexander to come here tonight, it will all be over tonight".* Shane was shocked saying, *"are you crazy, Mitchie? We can't do that, it's dangerous."* Mitchie says, *"we have to, we will end this tonight, ok?".* Shane says, *"fine, we will do this."* Mitchie heads to her room and changes before coming downstairs where Shane is waiting with her phone to record the message; Shane starts to film as Mitchie has a serious expression saying, *"Hey, Alexander! You think you have won? I am ready to face you! so you better come and face me! I am not afraid of you! I am still in my apartment, and I am ready to fight you! I have enough of your shitty games! So, let's end this! I will be waiting!."* Shane stops recording and sends it to Alexander as Mitchie asks, *"how was it?".* Shane replies, *"it's amazing! now we wait until the night has come".*

Mitchie thanks Shane saying, *"you are always here for me and always protect me, I am grateful for that… I can't do this without you."* Shane comes closer and holds her saying, *"hey, I will always be here for you, you don't have to worry, and I will do everything to keep you safe".* The rest of the day passes as Mitchie wakes up looking at the sky thinking, *'it's already night and still no sign of Alexander'.* She gets up looking for Shane as she comes into the kitchen which is empty just as a voice says, *"looking for me, Mitchie?".* Mitchie turns surprised saying, *"how did you get inside?!".* Alexander replies, *"I escaped once, remember?."* Just then Shane comes and punches him as he says, *"Mitchie, call the police!."* Mitchie says, *"on it!."* She grabs her phone thinking, *'I have to be quick!'.* Shane says, *"I won't let you touch or harm, Mitchie!".* Alexander says, *"playing the hero, huh?."* He takes out a gun and cocks it saying, *"YOU ARE GOING TO DIE!".* Mitchie turns to see Alexander pointing the gun at her as Shane notices this too but has no time to pull out his gun. He fires a shot as Shane drops to the floor with blood coming out of his body. Mitchie screams, *"NO!."* She bends down saying, *"Shane, no…..".* Mocco comes over and barks sadly as Alexander says, *"and now, it's your turn… Goodbye Mitchie".* Mitchie sees a gun in Shane's pocket and gets up saying, *"not today!".* She shoots him just as the front door opens and the cops arrive; Mitchie throws the gun and bends down beside Shane saying, *"please, get the ambulance, now! HURRY!."* Soon in the hospital Mitchie is waiting with Mocco as Joanna comes and sees them. She asks, *"what happened?!."* Mitchie replies, *"Alexander shot Shane."* Joanna says, *"no! I am sorry, Mitchie, I was the one who hired Alexander and it turned out that he was your stalker, it's all my fault isn't it? I hope you can forgive me."* Mitchie turns away and sees the doctor coming out of the operation theatre asking, *"doctor, how is Shane?".* The doctor replies, *"thank god, he's ok… he is strong and wants to live enough though he has lost a lot of blood".* Mitchie thanks the doctor as she asks, *"can I see him now?".* The doctor replies, *"It's better to give him a rest tonight but you can see him tomorrow".* Mitchie understands and leaves the hospital.

The next morning Mitchie comes with Darren to see Shane as she says, *"hey Shane".* Darren thanks Shane saying, *"thanks for taking care of my sister".* Shane says, *"my pleasure."* Mitchie asks, *"are you ok? I hope you are fine."* Shane insists he is okay and says, *"I am going to change and clean myself, then we can visit the police station".* Soon outside Darren asks, *"so are you going to see... this stalker in jail?".* Mitchie replies, *"yes, I need some answers."* Darren was reluctant just as a film crew called him back; Mitchie says, *"go complete your film!".* Darren hugged her and left as Shane came out ready to go.

Chapter 28

Soon in the car Mitchie shares her worries with Shane who stops the car and takes her hand saying, *"I love you Mitchie"*. Mitchie wipes her tears saying, *"you risked your life to protect me"*. Shane kisses her saying, *"not your life, my life... you are my life, Mitchie Torres"*. At the police station Mitchie and Shane see Alexander in the cell as he refuses to talk or co-operate. Soon after Shane brings Mitchie to a nearby café and buys her a latte and cupcake asking, *"hey, are you ok?"*. Mitchie replies, *"I don't know... I have still have some unanswered questions..."*. Shane says, "*don't dwell on the past, let's look forward to the future and now it's all over*". Mitchie smiles saying, *"I could never have done this without you"*. They share a kiss; a few months later Mitchie releases her album with Justin Timberlake, she also manages to get a role in a movie and despite everything her relationship with Shane is growing. One evening Shane prepares a special surprise for Mitchie on the beach which is a candlelight dinner; Mitchie enjoys the dinner as Shane takes her hand for a dance as Mitchie sees something glowing nearby in the sea. Mitchie sees the words '*Marry Me*.' She turns to Shane who is down on his knee saying, *"Mitchie Torres, I love you so much and I don't want to spend my life without you, will you marry me?"*. Mitchie has tears in her eyes and nods as he slips on the ring in her finger and lifts her in the moonlight as they share a passionate kiss. A few weeks later Mitchie is ready to get married as Joanna, Nala and Chloe are by her side; she comes out in her elegant white bridal dress as Darren says, *"I can't believe you are getting marry today, sis... I never imagine this day would come so soon"*. Mitchie says, *"don't cry!"*. Darren wipes his tears and hugs her saying, *"I am proud of you, Mitchie? Mom would be too"*. Mitchie says, *"love you, bro"*. Darren says, *"love you too, sis"*. Soon Darren brings Mitchie to the altar where Shane is waiting for her; Shane asks, *"are you nervous?"*.

Mitchie replies , *"no! never! I can't wait to marry you!"*. The priest is about to start as Shane says, *"may we...?"*. The priest nods as Shane says, *"Mitchie Torres, you are the person I want to spend forever with, I promise to protect you, love you and cherish you... always and forever, nothing can break us apart as I know that your love will always be my strength, you are my sunshine in life and the moon around my world, I love you Mitchie"*. Mitchie smiles as she says, *"I promise to always make you laugh, smile and be by your side, I am blessed to be standing here with you ready to start our lives together, I love you so much Shane Gray"*. The priest says, *"I now pronounce you husband and wife"*. They share a kiss as their friends and fans cheer on; Shane lifts her in his arms and carries her out. Later that night in their hotel room Mitchie says, *"I have a special gift for you"*. Shane replies, *"I don't need any gifts, I have the best one in front of me"*. Mitchie hands him a box as Shane is curious and opens it to see a pregnant test and a little pink baby dress reading, *'Baby Gray'*. Shane looks at Mitchie who smiles in delight as Shane comes over and lifts her saying, *"I LOVE YOU, Mitchie Gray"*. Mitchie kisses him saying, *"I love you too, Shane Gray"*. One year later, Mitchie and Shane's relationship is growing strong as Mitchie brings their baby daughter Kaitlyn to the beach for a special surprise; Darren and Chloe get married while Shane wonders, *'Mitchie has been acting strange... I hope everything is ok'*. As Mitchie raises a toast to the happy couple she says, *"I would also like to make a special announcement"*. Shane looks at Mitchie while holding their daughter as she says, *"our family of three is about to become a family of four"*. Everyone was surprised while Shane kissed Mitchie happily as Chloe gets up saying, *"our babies will be besties"*. She rubs her stomach gently as Darren kisses her happily saying, *"I love you so much, babe!"*.

Towards the end they all look at the sunset capturing a happy memory and brighter future to look forward to.

Milton Keynes UK
Ingram Content Group UK Ltd.
UKHW020729030823
426269UK00014B/544